MOUNTAIN LAUREL

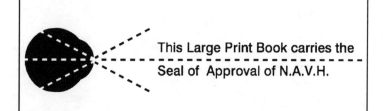

This Large Print Book carries the
Seal of Approval of N.A.V.H.

MOUNTAIN LAUREL

COLLEEN L. REECE

THORNDIKE PRESS

An imprint of Thomson Gale, a part of The Thomson Corporation

Detroit • New York • San Francisco • New Haven, Conn. • Waterville, Maine • London • Munich

THOMSON

✶

GALE

TM

Reece 10/06

LIBRARY OF CONGRESS CATALOGING-IN-PUBLICATION DATA

Reece, Colleen L.
  Mountain laurel / by Colleen L. Reece.
    p. cm. — (Thorndike Press large print Christian romance) (Wildflower harvest series ; no. 1) "Wildflower Harvest voted 3rd favorite historical romance by Heartsong Book Club Members. Has sequel: Desert Rose."
  ISBN 0-7862-8904-X (hardcover : alk. paper)
  1. Large type books. I. Title. II. Series: Reece, Colleen L. Wildflower harvest series ; no. 1 III. Series: Thorndike Press large print Christian romance series.
  PS3568.E3646M68 2006
  813'.54—dc22   2006017255

Published in 2006 by arrangement with Colleen L. Reece.

Printed in the United States on permanent paper
10 9 8 7 6 5 4 3 2 1

Say not ye, There are yet four months and then cometh harvest? behold, I say unto you, Lift up your eyes, and look on the fields; for they are white already to harvest.

John 4:35 (KJV)

ONE

Red Cedars shimmered with light and laughter. Carefully hoarded candles flickered and danced. Lamps held high to guide guests through the early autumn darkness cast a welcoming glow. Flames leaped and whirled in fireplaces. Not since the firing on Fort Sumter in the spring of 1861 that resulted in the formation of West Virginia had such an affair been held.

During the Civil War Thomas and Sadie Brown's farm, tucked into a fold of the Allegheny Mountains near Shawnee and the Virginia border, had somehow escaped detection by destroying Yankee troops. Neither had Rebel forces discovered the farm. Grateful, Thomas and Sadie shared what had been spared with those who had little or nothing. When in 1865 the War Between the States, a war of brother against brother, was officially resolved, new trials emerged: despair, starvation, and the need to begin again. Yet the Browns and others like them refused to be beaten. They started over or went on from where they were. The same pioneering spirit that created a new state brought them through tragedy. New lines of sorrow etched themselves on sturdy faces but their souls remained unwrinkled.

Now the Browns' home, Red Cedars, was host to a well-deserved celebration. September 1, 1873, felt centuries away from past misery. Without apology families wore their mended, treasured best; bonnets turned and freshened by determined, nimble fingers nodded. No one noticed or cared that curtains and portieres, damask tablecloths and napkins bore as battle scars cobwebby patches of darning.

In a secluded corner of the front room, made larger by open, dividing doors, Mountain Laurel Brown quietly observed the excited crowd. Still as the cool evening air, she caught sight of her older, married sisters. Blue-eyed Gentian was proudly displaying her new baby; Black-eyed Susan was flirting with her brand-new husband. A smile twitched Laurel's curved lips. Neighbors never had understood why Sadie Brown chose such outlandish names for her girls! But Laurel knew that beneath Sadie's starched corset cover and petticoats lived a heart made glad by beauty. Sadie could no more resist choosing flower names — and how well they fit — than she could allow muddy boots in the house.

A pang went through her. Although her older sisters both lived nearby, new homes and responsibilities claimed them. Mama said it was right and natural but Laurel missed them deeply.

"Stop it," she whispered to herself. "One of these days it will be your turn." She could feel her color rise from the modest round neck of her blue gown, up her white throat, and into her face. For pity's sake, why did she lurk here in this corner? Wasn't this also her twentieth birthday party?

She raised herself to her full five-foot, six-inch height and stretched her slim body. She took one step toward the crowd and paused, gazing across the room at her uncanny mirror image.

Large, dark brown, glowing eyes met hers. Light brown curls caught up in back to cascade to her shoulders shone in the light. Laurel objectively examined her reflection. A wide mouth and an upturned nose might be considered charming but they weren't beautiful.

The thought brought a wry twist to her mouth but, surprisingly, her image's smile remained sparkling. Even more amazing was that her identical dress had miraculously changed from forget-me-not blue to rosy pink!

Pride mingled with envy. Would she ever catch up with Ivy Ann who had been born five minutes before her and, in spite of her clinging name, managed to lead in everything the two girls had ever done?

Who cares, Laurel demanded of herself, but the uneven beat of her heart said otherwise.

I wish that for just one day, one week, one month, I could trade places with Ivy Ann, Laurel confessed silently. *How can two girls — no, women — look so much alike even Daddy and Mama mix us up yet be so different?*

She examined her twin's face and figure. Nothing there to separate them. Her gaze traveled to Ivy's head, cocked to one side while she listened to the praise heaped on her. High color made her especially lovely and again Laurel felt the familiar surge of pleasure that such an enchanting creature was a special part of herself.

"Laurel, what are you doing standing over here by yourself?" Thomas Brown's hearty voice boomed into her hideout. "Everyone's asking for you. Come on." With a large, work-worn hand he caught Laurel's small but sturdy one and led his daughter across the room.

"Where have you been?" Ivy Ann reproached. Vain, selfish, and thriving on admiration, the love she had for her twin matched Laurel's.

"What a pair!" someone called.

"Only problem is, how do you ever know which twin is which?" a young man muttered. A shout of laughter followed. Eligible suitors knew only too well how one could never be sure that Laurel and Ivy Ann weren't playing tricks.

Suddenly Laurel felt tired of it all. The wish to be herself and not just half of Ivy Ann almost choked her. Only her strong training received from determined parents kept her from bolting. Instead, she forced a smile and suffered herself to follow the wave of gaiety that tasted through supper and into the morning hours.

Even when she escaped she found no relief. The twins had shared a large room since babyhood. Laurel slowly removed her birthday present dress, brushed her hair, and climbed into bed. But Ivy Ann had been too tightly wound to run down yet.

"I am so glad Mama and Daddy encouraged us not to marry young," was her amazing remark once she emerged from the soft pink gown and slid into a ruffled nightdress.

Laurel couldn't help laughing. Trust Ivy Ann to come up with such a comment right on the heels of her splendid success at their party. "What made you think of that?"

"Oh, I don't know." She turned toward her twin. White teeth gleamed and the eyes that became provocative when a handsome neighbor appeared opened wide. "Gentian's baby is precious and Susan's husband is almost as wonderful as she thinks he is but I don't want to get married for ages and ages." Her smile melted some of Laurel's resistance. "I know we're considered old maids, but who cares?" She stretched white arms and yawned. "As long as there are men around to choose from, why marry? Are you willing to stay single until we're really old — twenty-five, maybe?"

"Mercy!" Laurel stared. "No man wants a wife that old."

A little frown marred Ivy Ann's forehead. "You're probably right, but my goodness, with all the nice young men coming to call, how can we ever make up our minds?"

Laurel refrained from reminding her twin how often those young men, even those who liked her, soon flitted from the quieter twin to the more daring, vivacious girl.

"Laurel, promise me that no matter who we marry or how far apart we may be, you won't ever let anything come between us."

Laurel sat up straight. Such serious conversation from Ivy Ann usually heralded some startling announcement. "Why would you want such a promise? What could come between us?"

"I don't know." Some of Ivy Ann's good mood had vanished. With troubled eyes, she stared at Laurel. "Sometimes I get the feeling we aren't as close as we used to be. Remember when we were small and always dressed exactly alike?" Nostalgia softened her face. "We don't now."

Laurel bit her lip. One of her small cries for freedom had brought about the change. "I like blue best and you like pink."

"I know, but somehow . . ." Ivy Ann's voice trailed and then died. "We don't like the same books or music either." Genuine sadness flickered in her eyes. "I just wish nothing had to change."

Understanding flooded Laurel. "You miss Gentian and Susan, don't you?"

"A lot more than I ever thought I would," she confessed with a quirk of her beautifully arched eyebrows. A deep dimple that had its counterpart in her sister's right cheek became obvious. "I thought I'd be glad when they left, they always bossed us around so. Especially Susan after Gentian married."

"Mama says she felt left out because we couldn't be separated."

Ivy Ann yawned and covered her mouth with her hand. "Perhaps. Anyway, now that we're women instead of girls we don't have younger sisters to boss! Too bad we don't have a brother." Her eyes gleamed. "They're mighty useful at bringing home young gentlemen."

"You are totally incorrigible," Laurel told her. "Goodnight."

"Goodnight."

Only after she heard her twin's soft breathing did Laurel remember she hadn't promised what Ivy Ann asked. Why should a strange feeling of relief fill her?

A week after the Browns' celebration Laurel sat mending on the wide front porch. The never-ending basket of household linens and clothing rested next to her rocking chair and her quick fingers stitched and wove until a second pile formed. Accustomed to the work, she could keep sewing and still enjoy the stately red cedars from which her home took its name. September continued to be beautiful. Only a faint touch of frost had come and leaves that in some years had cascaded in golden showers from hardwoods remained green.

From her viewpoint, Laurel could look down the sloped hillsides to the river below or up steeper hills to distant mountains. Daddy said when God created West Virginia he forgot to put in any flat land. She secretly rejoiced. How could people live where the country lay straight as a table top? Distant figures scrambling up and down ladders into laden apple trees foretold canning and cider making. Her fingers stilled. As much as she loved Red Cedars, an undefined longing deep inside touched her in quiet moments. Perhaps Ivy's foolish chatter about not marrying until they were twenty-five had triggered her melancholy. Or the look on Susan's face when her tall husband snatched her up and lifted her over the stile. The feeling that went through her when she held Gentian's baby or intercepted the flash of love between her sisters and their husbands was still very real.

"Please, God, I want to belong to *someone*." Her barely audible prayer shocked her. Proper young women didn't talk to God about such things, did they?

Why not? a small voice whispered in her heart. Every girl and young woman's dreams are important to God; anything that touches His creation interests Him.

A rush of skirts interrupted her new and thrilling reverie. "Out here mending and talking to yourself?" a lively voice demanded.

Laurel whipped around toward Ivy Ann and felt herself redden. "I thought you were making beds." Sadie Brown believed every girl must be head of her own household and know everything about housekeeping there was to know. "It's disgraceful how many southern girls can't do anything but flirt," she indignantly maintained, and churned faster one day when Ivy Ann complained about the work. "I'd be disgraced to have my daughters so helpless." Her lightning glance at Ivy brought a flush of shame to her cheeks.

"The day is long past when southern women have nothing to do but be petted and admired. If the South is ever to rise and regain her strength, it will take every man, woman, and child working together."

"I thought you were for the Union," Laurel teased.

Sadie's sharp eyes softened. "I am and always will be but that doesn't mean I'm not also a southern woman, just as my daughters will be if I have any say in the matter."

When Gentian and Susan went to their

own homes, they possessed every house-keeping skill known to their mother. Their husbands rejoiced and gave thanks, especially after hearing stories from friends who had married helpless southern belles!

"I made the beds." Ivy Ann flounced into a chair. "And dusted. And prepared a dessert for supper. All while you're out here enjoying the sunshine."

"Want to trade jobs?"

Ivy barely restrained a shudder. "Never. You know I hate mending." She broke off a late bloom from the fragrant rosebush that climbed up and over the porch roof. "Mmmmm. Smells good. That reminds me. We must have enough rose petals saved to scent our clothes."

Laurel's needle flashed silver in the sun. In and out, in and out, weaving together frayed edges. "There will also be enough to put in the soap." When Ivy Ann didn't answer, she glanced up. Her gaze followed her twin's down the road and up the hill that led to Shawnee. "What are you looking at?"

"Our fate."

Laurel dropped the needle. "Our *what?*" She looked at the empty lane then back at her sister, whose dreamy eyes were half-closed.

"Our fate. Can't you just see it? One of these days —" She dropped her voice to a mysterious tone. "Just when we least expect it, our fate will come riding down that hill and up the road. I wonder if we'll be ready for it."

"Are you stark, staring mad?" Laurel asked. "Whatever are you talking about?" Her pulse quickened in spite of her protest.

Ivy Ann dropped her indolent pose. Her eyes sparkled like dark molasses nuggets. She clapped her hands. "There is absolutely no romance in you, Mountain Laurel Brown! You should see as plainly as I that the most perfect young man God ever created is somewhere just waiting. When the time is right he will come riding, riding —"

Laurel's heart filled with mischief. " 'Oh, young Lochinvar is come out of the west. Through all the wide Border, his steed was the best. . . .' "

Ivy Ann drowned her out. " 'So faithful in love, and so dauntless in war, there never was knight like young Lochinvar.' " She rocked back and forth. "No Sir Walter Scott knight for me."

"Why not?" Laurel forgot her mending and concentrated on Ivy Ann. Not for a long time had the twins looked so alike with their teasing faces and hair loosened from good honest work. A vagrant breeze shook perfume from the roses and cooled the warm afternoon.

"Think I want to be carried off to who knows where, away from my family?" Ivy shook her head until her curls bounced. Some of the joy fled from her expressive face. "Could you stand having to live in some God-forsaken place, even with a husband?"

Laurel laughed outright. "West Virginia isn't the only place on earth, silly. What makes you think God has forsaken the rest of the world?"

"You know what I mean." Ivy Ann impatiently brushed aside the remark. A brooding look replaced her fun. "I never did care much for Ruth in the Bible."

"Ivy Ann, are you criticizing the *Bible*?" Laurel gasped.

"Don't be a ninny. I just don't see how she could promise to leave everything and go off down the road. Especially when it wasn't even with a husband, just a mother-in-law. A former mother-in-law, at that!" She glared at Laurel. "Don't tell me you could or would leave this and — and me."

Laurel silently considered it, while the breeze increased, rustled leaves, and flirted with the rosebush *Could she? Would she?*

19

Yet the Bible said husband and wife were to cleave to each other and never be parted in this life. She slowly said, "That's what the Bible tells us. God created man and woman to be so closely entwined they could face whatever hardships might come."

"Pooh! It's all very well to quote from the Bible but when it came right down to it, you couldn't leave Red Cedars except to settle real close, now could you?" Ivy Ann's eyes darkened until they looked almost black.

Laurel hedged. "You mean if you really and truly met a man you felt God wanted you to marry, you'd say no — even if you loved him and he loved you — unless he agreed to live in West Virginia?"

"Yes!" But an impish look crept over her face. "I just bet any man would be glad to stay around here if it meant marrying me." She leaned back in her chair and daintily crossed her soft white shoes.

"But what if his work were somewhere else?" Laurel couldn't drop the subject that had somehow become strangely significant to her. "What if he *had* to live elsewhere?"

"He'd have to make other arrangements," said Ivy Ann nonchalantly, dismissing the imaginary situation with a wave of her hand. "You still haven't answered my question."

For some reason she turned a little pale. "Would or would you not be a nineteenth-century Ruth?" Her clear voice hung in the ripening September air.

"I would." Laurel spoke from her innermost being. *Why did she feel the words committed her, like a solemn vow to something that would never happen?* "I would follow my husband wherever God called him to go." Her gaze never left Ivy's.

"Good for you!" Loud clapping followed the approving statement.

Laurel and Ivy Ann turned, torn from complete absorption in their discussion by the deep, masculine voice. A stranger stood on the bottom step, still applauding. Dark, interested eyes surveyed the twins. One fine hand held the reins of a spirited filly. Tall, straight, dark-haired and strong. . . .

There never was knight like young Lochinvar.

The words echoed in Laurel's brain. Laughter bubbled inside and to her horror escaped. Her dumbstruck twin just stared. But the stranger's dark eyes twinkled with merriment and Laurel couldn't help but wonder. The man had certainly come riding out of the west, down the hill and up their road. Could he possibly be the fate Ivy Ann predicted, stealing up while they talked, overhearing their girlish conversation?

And if so, whose fate might he prove to be? Two young women, one handsome man.

Laurel gasped. And in the split second before her twin recovered her wits enough to hold out her hand in greeting, Laurel thought, *I'm glad I didn't promise Ivy Ann what she wanted.*

TWO

"Dr. Birchfield?" The plain-faced, middle-aged woman who came in daily to clean his cottage and office tapped lightly at the open door.

Adam raised his head from the medical journal he had stolen time to read. "Yes?" Although his mind stayed on the report of new advances in treating contagious disease, his alert eyes caught the telltale twisting of Mrs. Cutler's hands.

Her firm mouth trembled. "Is it true, what they say? That you'll be leaving Concord soon?" Before he could stifle his amazement and answer, the good woman added, "Why, Birchfields have lived in Massachusetts as far back as anyone can remember. None ever wanted to live anywhere else, until —" She broke off and dull red suffused her face.

"Until my older brother Nathaniel refused to fight in a war he hated and left home," Adam grimly finished. He set his lean jaw and his dark eyes flashed. "Where did you hear that I might be leaving?"

"I couldn't help overhearing you argue, er, your discussion with your father this morning." She stared at the floor then looked straight into Adam's furious face. "Begging your pardon, Doctor, but Jeremiah and Patience have already lost one son. Surely you won't desert them too."

Only strong regard for Mrs. Cutler's long, well-meaning friendship kept back the hot words that sprang to Adam's lips. "I'd appreciate it if you keep what you heard to yourself," he told her. "I don't know what I'm going to do — yet."

Mrs. Cutler sighed. "You'll have to do what you think's right. Every tub has to stand on its own bottom. But isn't there a way for you and your father to part without anger if you feel you must go?"

Adam didn't reply and Mrs. Cutler vanished from the doorway, leaving him more disturbed than he cared to be. He stood, walked to the window open to an early August afternoon, and stared unseeingly into the perfect day that at another time would have enticed him outside.

Without anger — if only it could happen! He could not deny the restlessness that had filled him ever since he finished medical training and returned to Concord. Had it started when his father exploded at his idea of setting up a separate office when Jeremiah had long planned that Adam would join him in practice?

First Nat, then me. Adam drummed his fingers on the white-painted windowsill. The admission opened Pandora's box. Memories Adam wished he could forget crowded into the sunny room.

From the time he could toddle Adam worshiped his brother Nathaniel. He followed after him, never realizing until he grew up how unusual it was for a boy six years older to suffer the presence of a small child and make him feel welcome. Jeremiah and Patience looked with approval on the boys' relationship. Dr. Birchfield's dream of having Nathaniel march in his own steps inspired Adam. Someday he too would study medicine. How wonderful if all three of them could work together!

Like a thunderbolt came news of war with the South. No man in New England carried the fire of patriotism higher than Jeremiah Birchfield. He could not volunteer because of a heart problem, but his face flamed when he summoned twenty-year-old Nathaniel home from his medical training in early 1862.

"I can't go, but I proudly send my best, my oldest son."

Patience, whose name matched her God-fearing personality, wrung a fine handkerchief mercilessly but made no protest. She seldom took a stand against her rock-ribbed husband. His streak of granite resembled those found in the stern New England hills.

Adam, whose fourteenth birthday had just passed, started to speak. A single glance from Nathaniel quelled his words. The next instant Nat spoke.

"I am sorry to disappoint you, Father, but I cannot go."

Patience's nervous fingers stilled.

Adam could only stare at the white radiance in his adored brother's face.

Jeremiah rose to full height, towering in his shock and disbelief. "What is this foolishness? You *must* go."

"I cannot."

"To think I would see the day my own son turned coward and refused to fight for his country!"

Jeremiah's rage brought misery to Nathaniel's dark eyes but his steady gaze didn't even flicker. "I am no coward. I cannot fight in a war I don't believe should happen." He warmed to his subject, given opportunity by his father's stunned silence.

"Don't you see? The North condemns the South for slavery. Yet how many families living here keep colored servants?"

Speechless, Jeremiah raised a warning hand but Nat rushed on.

"If I thought this conflict was about preserving the Union or bringing equality to all people, it would be different." The fight went from him. A beseeching look replaced his determination. "Father, please, if you can't understand, at least respect my decision."

Adam held his breath, silently praying for God to do something, anything.

Jeremiah got his second wind. Anger overrode reason. "As long as I furnish you with meat and drink and shelter you will obey me. I say you will put aside these blasphemous ideas and serve the country your forefathers sought to be free and worship God." Every word beat into the room with the force of a physical blow.

Patience roused from her submissiveness. *"Don't do this!"* She ran to her husband and caught his arm. The strings of the morning cap she wore loosened.

"Woman, be still."

"I will not be still!" she cried. "He's our son, yours and mine. Nothing can ever change that."

"He has changed it of his own free will," Jeremiah stormed. "Nathaniel Birchfield, if you refuse to do a man's duty, you are hereafter no son of mine."

"Jeremiah, *no!*" Patience burst into mournful weeping.

"It's all right, Mother. Father may not claim me as a son but he can't stop me from loving him. I am truly sorry."

When Nat marched from the room Adam choked. His brother's shoulders squared in such an erect position Adam had the feeling Nat stepped to the sound of martial music only he could hear.

That same afternoon Nathaniel left Concord. "Don't blame Father too much," he told his brokenhearted brother. "Someday, when the war is over, perhaps he will change." He tousled Adam's raven hair, so like his own. "Try and make up for me if you can. Godspeed."

While the war raged and Patience and Adam grieved, Jeremiah Birchfield permitted no mention of Nathaniel's name. He could not control his younger son's thoughts though. Adam held tight to a dream that one day, when he had the resources, he would find Nat. Years and miles meant nothing compared with the brother enshrined in Adam's heart. A few scattered letters came. Twice Jeremiah saw them first and tore them into bits without reading them. The others told little except that Nat was well and had worked at everything from being a farmer to a blacksmith. He also wrote he missed his family.

Adam took a deep breath and held it. When it rushed out he turned back to the desk, his mind still turbulent. "I've been faithful, Nat," he said half under his breath. "I became a doctor as Father wished. But I'm twenty-five years old now. You're thirty-one. Lately I feel you need me." The same prickle that had caused the earlier argument with Jeremiah returned. A trivial comment had slipped out in spite of Adam's guarded tongue.

"I'll wager that if Nat had become a doctor he'd be a far better one than I." He instantly clamped his mouth shut but it was too late.

"I know no Nathaniel and if you are as wise as you ought to be you'll do the same."

Adam had learned patience and pity for the father who had aged so in the past eleven years. Yet he had also inherited Jeremiah's quick temper and his own sense of justice. "Father, why can't you forget the past? I've heard you read stories from the Bible about the need to forgive —"

"Are you daring to tell me what to do?" Slumbering fires fed by guilt and stubbornness flared.

Adam shook his head. "No, I just know how much Mother misses Nathaniel. If you can't forgive him for yourself and for him, can't you do it for Mother's sake?"

Jeremiah's features turned to chiseled marble. "I believe you had something you wished to consult me about?"

Adam's despair at his family's estrangement caused him to lose control. He clenched his hands and said slowly, "I want to leave Concord."

Suspicion reddened the old doctor's face. "You're not considering going after — him?"

Adam had never lied in his life. Nat had taught him from babyhood that lies and deceit lead to dishonor. Of all the sins, Adam learned to despise dishonesty most.

"Someday." Before Jeremiah could answer he added, "Besides, I'd like to take my medical skills where they'd do more good than here in Concord."

"Perhaps to the Wyoming Territory?" His father's loaded question confirmed Adam's belief that Jeremiah had kept far more careful track of Nat than anyone realized.

"Perhaps."

"You'd give up all you have here, a secure practice, the respect of the town, the chance to prosper. . . ." Jeremiah's face grayed.

"Father, didn't you and Mother come to Concord not knowing what it held, not sure if you could establish a practice here?" Adam spread his hands out, palms up. "Look at these hands. They are skilled in surgery and caring for the sick but they aren't needed here. You and Dr. Partridge can handle things while I'm gone."

"And how long is that to be?" Jeremiah folded his arms in a gesture that warned Adam the discussion was not settled.

"I don't know."

Jeremiah grunted. "I thought so. Adam, if you walk away from everything I've given you —" He hesitated. Did he remember another gauntlet thrown down to a son who had no choice but to pick it up? "We'll discuss this later." He strode away, his shoulders slumped but still determined.

No wonder Mrs. Cutler's plea haunted him, Adam thought. The arrival of afternoon patients and several calls on horseback swerved his mind from the problem. *How old and tired and ill Jeremiah looked. Could his one remaining son leave him, even for the best of reasons?*

"Dear God, what shall I do?" Adam reverted to his usual way of solving problems. "Go? Stay? Or merely wait?" When no answer flashed into his brain and heart he decided God's signal must be to wait.

It didn't take long. A few days later Jeremiah Birchfield commanded Adam to come for supper and startled both wife and son with an announcement. "You've been wanting to see what medical practice out in the wilds is like. Can you be ready to leave tomorrow morning?"

"Leave? For where?" Adam put down his fork and swallowed his last bite of molasses-sweetened apple pie.

"West Virginia." Satisfaction oozed from the older man's entire being. "I have it all arranged. You'll visit mountain areas where everything you've learned will war with the conditions you find there. You will see poverty and squalor, superstition and apathy until you'll be ready to come back and appreciate Concord."

Adam ran the full gamut of emotions: anger at his father's high-handed disposal of himself; unwilling interest and a sense of adventure; compassion for his wide-eyed mother; even amusement at Jeremiah in foiling his plan to head West.

"I can be ready." Adventure had won, but the war between father and son had not ended. This trip to West Virginia was simply the first skirmish between them.

Adam's departure had to be postponed a day. Such a furor over his going ensued that Jeremiah gruffly said, "Wait until tomorrow. The neighbors are determined to bid you Godspeed." A dazed Adam was only half aware of the impromptu covered dish supper, an expression of the townspeople's regard. Not surprisingly, his leaving rekindled village gossip of years before about where "that ungrateful Nathaniel Birchfield" had ended up. Adam stumbled onto one such conversation and effectively stopped it with one steady look at the offenders.

He secretly rejoiced when everyone left and he could go back to the cottage for his last night there. When would he see it again? Despite what Jeremiah thought, Adam instinctively knew all the miseries he faced in West Virginia wouldn't send him running for home like a whipped dog.

"Dear God," he wondered aloud, "Is this the first step toward Nat?" The soft night wind blew in from the west and brought cooling relief, and an invitation. He wished he could have gone that morning instead of having to wait. Yet the next day he gave thanks to God it had not been so. Just before he locked his cottage door for the last time, Patience Birchfield's hired girl rushed up to him. From the folds of her voluminous apron she pulled a letter that showed stains of travel. "Miz Patience says take it." She scurried away just before Jeremiah arrived.

Adam quickly pocketed the worn letter. His heart pounded from the glimpse of bold writing and it took all his concentration not to betray himself to his father.

"I'll be expecting reports of your work." Eyes undulled by age and heartache bore into Adam.

"I'll write. I promise." The younger doctor held out a slim hand and grasped the other's lined one.

"Godspeed." After a moment Jeremiah added, "Son."

"Godspeed, Father." Other words trembled on his lips but refused to form. Adam watched his father turn away heavily and walk down the road toward the red-brick traditional house that had been built a few years after the Birchfields came. Jeremiah didn't look back. If agony and the same uncertainty of father and son meeting again in this life touched him as it did Adam, no one knew.

The trip by rail to West Virginia always

remained a blur in Adam's mind. Enthralled by the long letter Nathaniel had sent, irretrievably caught by the older man's plea for him to consider coming West, Adam's eyes saw the changing country but his heart and mind could not take them in. Snatches of the letter haunted him.

Medical help is practically nonexistent.

It will come as a great surprise, I am sure, but I made the greatest decision of my life a little over a year ago.

I feel God has called me to be His servant. After much prayer and study, I have accepted a tough assignment and am building a church in the small but wild hamlet of Antelope in the rugged Wind River Range of the Rocky Mountains.

Here will I live, serve — and one day lie.

How much you could do, if you came.

. . .

The next days and weeks tore at Adam. Father had been right: Many of the West Virginians struggled and overcame, but some did not. Bound by tradition and mountain superstition, bereaved and desolated by heavy losses of both family members and crops, Adam found he had more to do than three doctors could handle. The old doctor who should have retired years before demanded and got a fine horse for Adam. Beyond that and his food and shelter, Adam received little. Yet mountain-proud patients gave what they had, simply and quietly — a haunch of venison, turnips, apples, and once, a worn but still usable quilt.

At first Adam protested but his host soon stopped that. "Everything's been taken from them but their pride. Tuck yours away in your pocket and let them keep theirs," he advised when Adam insisted the families needed things more than he.

August ended and September slipped in. One beautiful afternoon Adam found himself free for the first time since he came to the hills.

"I don't know quite how to act," he confessed to his good mentor.

"Now if I were forty or so years younger and had a free day, I'd ride out and say thanks to the folks who donated that filly." The mountain doctor's eyes twinkled. "Being it's such a nice day and all."

Adam distrusted the twinkle but eagerly snatched the idea. He'd sent thanks but wanted to let the generous family know how much he appreciated the loan. The filly's easy stride gobbled up miles and Adam had found to his amazement that he was a natural horseman.

Adam wiped his face from the burning September sun and recognized from Doc's directions the lane he sought. A flash of blue from the wide porch showed someone was home. A little hesitantly, he rode closer to the house, dismounted, and paused with one foot on the bottom step. Cool vines and a climbing rose offered no obstruction to the clear voices.

Amused, Adam listened to the spirited discussion just beyond the climbing rose.

"Would you or would you not be a nineteenth-century Ruth?" a light voice demanded.

"I would. I would follow my husband wherever God called him to go."

Why should the rich voice send joy through Dr. Adam Birchfield? "Good for you!" he called and applauded.

Not one but two bewitching young women whirled to face him. Then the one in blue laughed, and Adam thought of bubbling water.

THREE

Dedicated to medicine and determined to learn everything he could, Adam Birchfield had wasted no time on romance. When he saw a particularly attractive woman, a vague realization that one day he'd have to find a wife pierced his studies. He laughed then reassured himself that when that time came God would provide. His fellow medical students jeered at the idea.

"God? Why, He's busy enough keeping this old world from going to ruin. How can you expect Him to be a matchmaker?"

"I don't." But Adam grinned and laughter lurked in his dark eyes. "You have to admit, though, getting married is one of the biggest events in a man's life. I talked with God about becoming a doctor. Why not about marriage?"

"You sound like a parson," his chief rival for top honors accused. "Maybe you should have gone into preaching."

"I thought of it." Adam raised one eyebrow. "But I believe no one should take that honor unless called of God and I feel no such call." He yawned. "Enough talking. I have one tough examination first thing in the morning."

Even when he completed his training and became established in Concord, Adam shied away from the droves of young women who hounded him. Something fine inside refused to succumb to those who set traps for him and generally were nuisances. Once he exploded to his father, "Why can't they see real men can't abide their silliness?" His face softened. "Mother isn't like that and I bet she never was."

A poignant look of remembrance touched Jeremiah's craggy features. "Patience lived and continues to live up to the Proverbs description of what a godly woman and wife should be. My boy, no man has ever had a better companion." As if regretting the moment, he snapped, "Now let's get back to business. Have you convinced old man Trescott to let you treat him or is he still insisting on seeing me?"

They launched into a medical discussion but Adam's heart warmed to his father in a way it had seldom done since Nat left.

Now a pair of dark eyes — no, two pairs

of dark eyes — haunted him. Sadie Brown issued an invitation for the visiting doctor to have supper with them and Ivy Ann prettily concurred. Laurel's quiet look convinced him. Before Adam remounted to ride back to Doc's, he had accepted further invitations to drop by any time he could.

The second time he came ended with a discussion of the opportunities out West.

"Is it true that women are really allowed to vote and to hold office in the Wyoming Territory?" Thomas might be a farmer but he loved to keep up on events outside his own domain. His eyes glistened.

So did Laurel's. When Ivy Ann whispered, "Who cares?" her sister whispered back fiercely, "I do! Be still and listen, will you?" Ivy's eyes opened wide like a spanked kitten's but she acquiesced.

"My brother Nathaniel writes that it's all true." Adam glowed with pride. He had sketched in why Nathaniel went West, surprised and pleased that the Browns bore no resentment toward a northerner who wouldn't fight. He had also shared how Nat wandered until he came to a point where he truly believed God wanted him to serve as a minister. Nat chose Antelope in the opening territory because, Adam quoted his brother, " 'The fields are white already to harvest.' "

"He sounds terribly good to me," Ivy Ann put in.

Adam glanced at her sharply but her innocent face gave no sign of criticism, only admiration.

"Tell us more." Sadie echoed Laurel's unspoken plea. "What about Indian trouble? And women's voting rights?" Her eyes snapped. "About time wives and mothers were allowed to have a say."

"Mama's all for women being given the vote." Ivy Ann couldn't keep out of the conversation long. "So's Laurel." She shot a look of mischief toward her twin.

"How about you?"

Ivy Ann covered a dainty yawn with slender fingers. "Dear me, I'm not sure I could choose." A shout of laughter followed but Adam took her seriously.

"Just surviving in a new and untamed land is hard. The women work alongside their men and bear children as well." He saw the shocked look that passed between the girls. "I ask forgiveness if I'm indelicate, but as a doctor I see the bearing of children as natural." He quickly changed the subject. "About women voting, Congress created the Territory of Wyoming in 1868 and in

1869 the Wyoming Territorial Legislature gave women the right to vote and hold elected office. In 1870, Esther H. Morris became the nation's first woman justice of the peace."

Inspired by all but Ivy Ann's rapt attention, Adam went on, quoting from Nathaniel and from everything he had read, in fact all he could find about the new western frontier.

"Lieutenant John Fremont explored the Wind River Mountains way back in 1842 and 1843 but fur trade began just after 1800. Over the years it resulted in the Indian wars we've heard about. But the discovery of gold in the 1860s in Montana triggered off trouble."

"Then you'll be going into danger?" Wide-eyed, Ivy Ann leaned forward, making a pretty picture in the firelight and softly shaded lamplight.

Adam shook his head, "No, Red Cloud and other Indian leaders signed a treaty about five years ago. They agreed not to interfere with the building of the Union Pacific Railroad in southern Wyoming in exchange for the army's abandonment of Fort Phil Kearney and two other forts. This gave northeastern Wyoming back to the Indians who hated this fort." Doubt filled

Adam's eyes. "Nat says it's an uneasy truce and peace."

Laurel spilled over. "I don't blame the Indians at all! If reports are true, they've been lied to again and again."

"All the more reason for Nat to establish a church in Antelope. He hopes not only to reach the cowboys and miners and ranchers in that area, but perhaps take the Gospel to the Indians."

"You are really going, aren't you?" Ivy Ann asked. "But what about your wife? Will she leave Massachusetts and live in this place called Antelope?"

"Wife!" Adam's hearty laugh filled the room and brought answering smiles to the others' faces. "I have no wife. Anyway, what decently brought up girl would give up everything and trail along with me to such an untried country? Would you?" He looked deep into Ivy Ann's dark eyes.

Ivy wrinkled her nose in disgust. "Go out where there's nothing but cowboys and miners and ranchers?"

"Oh, there are other things," Adam said solemnly. "Jackrabbits and mule deer, elk and black bears. There are grizzly bears and mountain lions, lynxes and coyotes, foxes, skunks, and wildcats."

"Please, no more!" Ivy covered her ears.

"I haven't even begun." Adam's excitement knew no bounds and lighted fires of interest in the others. "We mustn't forget the fur animals such as beavers, raccoons, martens, and otters. Or the pronghorns —"

"What's a pronghorn?" Ivy Ann took down her hands and pouted. "Another dangerous animal?"

"They're like a deer and like an antelope and roam the Rocky Mountain plains area by the thousands. Nat says they're so beautiful they make his throat hurt. Tan with dark markings and short black horns, their varied coloration protects them by blending into their surroundings.

"You know, the Wyoming Territory has flat land *and* towering peaks and rugged canyons, racing rivers *and* waterfalls."

"I've heard that it's dreadfully cold." Ivy Ann shivered.

"In winter, yes, but a dry cold that men can stand." Adam breathed deeply.

"Men, but not women." Ivy Ann tossed her curly head. "Why don't you just settle around here? There's plenty of need for a new doctor." She smiled provocatively. "Lots of pretty girls, too, and, as you said, no decently brought up girl would go out there with you —"

"I would." Laurel said. Then red blood

flooded her smooth skin. "I mean, that is, not with Dr. Birchfield, but if I were in love with someone. . . ."

For the second time in their acquaintance something passed between Adam and the quiet twin who had so bravely spoken out. For a single instant a feeling of kinship existed before being suddenly shattered by Ivy Ann's laughing accusation.

"You know you'll marry someone right around here, Laurel, so don't sound all noble! You couldn't bear to be away from Shawnee more than a few miles, any more than I could." She gracefully rose, linked her arm in Laurel's, and pulled her to her feet. The twins' wide, soft skirts rustled and swayed with the movement.

"See, Dr. Birchfield? You don't really think young women like us should go to the Wyoming Territory, do you?"

Adam's heart plummeted and he silently called himself a fool. After twenty-five years of walking alone, why should the impossibility of such a thing affect him? He stood, better able to think while on his feet. He paused in the way he had of thinking before ever committing himself. When he spoke it came from a belief that had crystallized while reading and rereading Nathaniel's letters.

"Miss Brown," Adam's gaze turned from Ivy Ann to Laurel. "Whether Christian young women such as you *would* go to the Wyoming Territory I have no way of knowing. But yes, I believe such women *should.* Without decent women to establish and maintain homes and schools and churches, wild and lawless men can only live rough lives, shorn of the beauty only women can provide. Nathaniel says the few wives who have accompanied their mates are already making a difference. They are almost worshiped by those very men who shoot and gamble!"

Undaunted, Ivy Ann tossed her head again. "I've heard the women in the West are — are —" She struggled to find an acceptable but significantly telling word. "Are bad," she finished triumphantly.

Adam folded his arms and looked stern. "There will always be bad women and men as long as strong Christian followers balk at inconvenience, danger, and hardship." He clamped his lips into a straight line then deliberately smiled, hoping to erase the impression of criticism. "I must go. I am grateful for your warm southern hospitality. We who live in the North should be so gracious."

"Goodnight, Dr. Birchfield." Ivy Ann

extended one hand and clung to her twin with the other. "Perhaps your mission *is* to convince certain Christian followers. Do come again."

Adam hid a grin. He had nettled this young woman more than she cared to admit. He bowed over her hand, then Laurel's. "If time permits, I will." He turned toward Thomas and Sadie. "Forgive me for monopolizing the conversation. I never could resist Nat's enthusiasm. As soon as I finish my promised stay here I plan to go West." He smiled. "I frankly admit I'm glad I can ride the Union Pacific across country. I'm not yet skilled enough at horseback riding to relish the thought of traveling that way."

In true southern custom, the Browns accompanied Adam outside. Thomas insisted on helping him saddle the filly and all four stood in the cool night air until the sound of hoofbeats dwindled and faded into distant silence.

"He's a bit of a crusader, isn't he?" Ivy Ann flounced inside and away from her family's protest. "Can you imagine?" She folded her arms and said in a passable imitation of Adam's pronouncement, *"Whether Christian young women such as you would go to Wyoming I have no way of knowing. But yes, I believe such women should. . . ."* She broke off and mirthfully grasped her sides. "For pity's sake, deliver me from earnest young men!" Still laughing, she lightly ran upstairs.

Laurel felt reluctant to follow. The entire evening had quickened her senses as nothing had done before. Before Adam Birchfield's arrival the vague sense of wanting something more than her present way of life had smoldered. The intense young doctor had fueled her discontent. She also remembered his challenging words. Not lightly, as did Ivy Ann, but in a way that she couldn't fully comprehend.

Her own faltering explanation flashed into her mind like a sunrise over mountains. "I mean, that is, not with Dr. Birchfield, but if I were in love with someone. . . ."

Laurel slowly climbed the stairs, treasuring the surprised and admiring glance Adam had given her, the feeling of kinship. Even Ivy Ann had been excluded from that moment. If only he were staying longer, perhaps the fragile thread could strengthen. She sighed and reached the top of the stairs then walked down the hall to her room and to Ivy Ann.

Laurel's heartfelt wish changed in the short time before Adam Birchfield went

West and out of her life forever. Obviously piqued by the way the doctor had at first equally divided his attention between the twins, Ivy pulled out every trick from her enormous store of enticements. A soft hand laid on Adam's arm when it wasn't necessary. The cocked head and intense concentration on what he said. Downcast eyes followed by a quick upward sweep of long lashes over melting brown eyes.

Laurel secretly raged, angry with Ivy Ann and even more furious with herself. None of the tricks was new. She just hated seeing them used on Adam. "He's too fine for cheapness," she whispered to herself, then wondered why she cared.

Yet she quietly rejoiced the day Ivy Ann overstepped herself. Clad in one of Laurel's favorite blue gowns, the scheming young woman met Adam at the door, made up an excuse about her sister not feeling well, and prepared to keep Adam to herself. She didn't identify herself as Laurel but neither did she act like Ivy Ann. A half-hour later when a perfectly healthy and unsuspecting Laurel came into the big living room calling, "Ivy Ann, Mama wants us," she met Adam's shocked gaze.

"How do you like my little trick?" Ivy Ann asked Adam, but Laurel saw her twin's fingers tremble in the folds of the blue gown.

"I find deceit in any form totally abominable. It is nice that your sister has recovered — so rapidly."

Ivy Ann turned crimson and cast a resentful glance at Laurel who just stood there.

"Miss Brown, may I have the pleasure of your company while getting my horse?" Adam asked Laurel.

"Oh, we'll both go with you." Ivy Ann tucked her hand under his arm in the way that never failed to obtain forgiveness.

Adam didn't unbend. "Miss Brown?" He offered his other arm to Laurel who felt torn between wanting to laugh and ignoring Ivy's glare. Flanked by the young women, so alike and yet so opposite, Adam reached his horse, bowed, and rode off "stiffer than Mama's starched petticoats," Ivy Ann complained. Unholy glee filled Laurel. If they never met another man Ivy couldn't twine around her finger, at least Adam Birchfield hadn't succumbed to Ivy's tricks.

Adam only had time to visit once more. Several times Laurel caught his glance resting on her but, as usual, Ivy Ann kept herself on center stage. Never had she been more vivacious and lovely, bewildering and changeable as in a rosy gown that modestly left visible only a little round of white neck and dimpled hands below her ruffled sleeves. If she felt embarrassment or contrition over Adam's last visit, even Laurel couldn't see it. By mutual agreement, neither twin had told their parents what happened. Thomas and Sadie well knew their daughter's ways but Laurel never carried tales and Ivy seldom confessed anything that would mar her image.

Adam appeared restless and Laurel knew how eager he must be to get going. When Ivy vanished for a few minutes he shared his heart's concern. "It's close to twelve years. I wonder if Nathaniel and I will have to get acquainted all over. There's a lot of difference between twenty and almost thirty-two."

"No more than between fourteen and more than twenty-five," Sadie reminded. She patted the young doctor's hand. "The same love you and your brother shared while he lived at home is there." She pointed to the fireplace, well banked for the night. "See?" Sadie tossed a twig and flames shot out to snatch it greedily. "That's all it will take."

Laurel watched Adam's bowed head and saw his throat work. God grant that he would find his brother well. Envy swept through her. If she were a man she would do as Adam Birchfield had chosen to do — go where decent, law-abiding people could make a difference. But Daddy and Mama would never agree to her going West. *Unless you married someone who lived there,* a little voice said inside.

Glad for once of Ivy's renewed chatter Laurel silently enjoyed the final minutes of Adam's company. *Why did she have to be so tongue-tied? Why couldn't she be more like her twin?* Yet even her special love for Ivy Ann couldn't blind her to the fact Adam simply hadn't fallen at her sister's small feet. His voice remained the same when he bid each of them goodbye.

"May God go with you," Thomas said when he gripped Adam's hand. "I almost wish I were going too."

Laurel saw the way Adam's hand tightened and the blaze in his face. "Perhaps, sir, one day you will."

"Leave Red Cedars?" Thomas acted surprised yet something in his face when he turned toward his wife and daughters sent a strange spurt of hope through Laurel. What if they did go West, all of them, in spite of Ivy Ann's fretting? Her traitorous heart skipped a beat then rushed on. The prospect of seeing Adam Birchfield again sent flags flying in her cheeks and in her heart.

FOUR

Every mile of the long journey between Shawnee, West Virginia, and Antelope, Wyoming Territory, strengthened Adam Birchfield's belief in the rightness of his decision. Every mile proved a revelation to the once provincial young man who had been born, raised, and schooled in Massachusetts. Not until his West Virginia odyssey had Adam seen anything other than his own state or been on his own. At home and school Jeremiah dominated. In West Virginia the good old mountain doctor took a father's place. The intoxicating allure of freedom flowed in Adam's veins and consumed his every thought.

With every mile he thanked God for this opportunity and asked for Jeremiah's eventual forgiveness. At times he felt remorseful over the way he had sent news of his departure too late for his father to respond. Yet what good would more arguments have done except to worsen things between father and son? Better to follow Mrs. Cutler's advice and go without more anger. Mother must never again be forced to stand by helplessly and see a son cast out.

Adam thrilled to the ever-changing scenes that fled past his window seat. Rolling hills gave way to gentle farmlands; cities that had meant little more than a test of memory in geography sprang into solid, unforgettable places. Time after time he marveled. How could even the sturdiest pioneer have traveled the weary miles, walking behind covered wagons that stirred up dust? A little pang went through him. How many of those same men, women, and children lay beneath the prairie sod, mute witnesses to the settling of the West? A little prayer of gratitude filled his heart.

He resented the darkness, boyishly afraid he would miss something. As long as twilight showed even the most open, empty land, Adam strained his eyes to see. "I may never be here again," he whispered then straightened, shocked at himself. Had he so fallen in love with Nathaniel's West he was ready to disown the East forever? Impossible! Mother, Father, everything he knew lay waiting in Massachusetts.

Yet across the grassy plains, beyond the

distant mountains, the unseen hamlet of Antelope in all its wildness had already stacked a claim in his heart.

I will probably be the only doctor for hundreds of miles, he admitted. *How can I care for patients in such circumstances?* He had prayed that his skills might be used. If all he expected came to pass, God's answer to his prayer could be overwhelming!

Even while Adam glued his gaze to outside the window, his mind and heart remembered Red Cedars. There was Ivy Ann, shallow but charming. Did a sound, true heart beat underneath all the frills? He closed his eyes and a rosy vision danced before him. A man could find excitement enough for a lifetime if he could get beyond the southern belle pose and reach Ivy's heart.

An involuntary smile crossed his face at the thought of Laurel. At first he had found her a quieter version of Ivy Ann. Adam shook his head. Laurel's passionate outbursts about leaving all to cleave unto her mate had turned her glowing dark eyes to almost-black. A lot of banked fire burned within the sometimes-overlooked twin. What if Thomas and Sadie answered the call of the West? Thomas's excitement when they discussed it betrayed an untamed, pioneer spirit. What an asset that family would be to Antelope!

Adam awoke to a gradual slowing of the train as it climbed. Rubbing the sleep from his eyes, he looked straight out at snow-capped peaks he wouldn't have believed existed outside of an artist's rendering. Amazingly, even though the train steadily chugged on for hours, the peaks came no closer!

A grizzled man with well-worn boots and an oversized hat laughed at Adam's astonishment. "Son, out here the air is so clear things look a powerful lot closer. Are you aimin' to stay?"

"Yes, at least for a while." Adam threw a sop to his conscience.

Shrewd eyes measured the young doctor. "Let me give you a word of advice. Never hop on a cayuse and head out toward the mountains — or anywhere — without findin' out from someone who knows how far you have to go."

"Thanks." Adam felt humbled before this man's direct concern and friendliness.

"How come an easterner like you is in the Wyomin' Territory?"

"Why, my brother is here. I'm a doctor and he asked me to come."

"A *doctor?*" The rancher clapped Adam on the shoulder so hard the younger man nearly fell out of his seat. "That's a whole bushel of good news. Where you aimin' to settle?"

"In Antelope." Adam regained some of his composure. "My brother's building a church there and —"

"Jumpin' grasshoppers, if you ain't Nat Birchfield's brother!" The welcoming grin accompanied another backslap but this time Adam braced himself. He could feel his blood pound in his head.

"You know Nat?" he asked eagerly.

"Half of Wyomin' Territory knows him and admires what he's doin' to help make Antelope a place for decent folks to live and raise their families." His unqualified approval warmed Adam to the tips of his travel-stained shoes.

"My name's Hardwick." He thrust out a weather-beaten hand in the kind of grip Adam expected from such a man. "I own the Lazy H spread a few miles out of Antelope. Run quite a few cattle and horses."

What luck! Adam leaned forward and his dark eyes flashed. "I don't mean to pry but how many is 'quite a few?' "

Hardwick grinned again. "Consider'ble more than last year, maybe less than next year." He laughed outright at Adam's raised eyebrow and relented. "We drove a bunch of cattle rustlers out of the country about a year ago so the Lazy H and other ranches are prosperin'." His eyebrows pulled together and the corners of his mouth turned down. "Who knows what kinda varmints will come creepin' back? Or if the good Lord will choose this year for a ripsnorter of a winter that freezes critters where they stand? Then there's the little matter of hail and drought, flood and fire from lightnin'." He jerked his big hat down over his eyes and mumbled, "Man's a fool to try and beat this crazy country."

"But you wouldn't live anywhere else." Adam's newly gained wisdom prompted the comment.

Hardwick shoved his hat to the back of his grizzled head. Adam caught the same approval in his eyes that had been there when they discussed Nat. "Reckon you're goin' to be all right out here." For the second time he pulled his hat forward. A few minutes later snores rumbled in time with the train wheels.

There was no sleep for Adam. Hardwick had given him — a tenderfoot — the highest possible compliment. Too bad Ivy Ann Brown couldn't hear Hardwick. What had he said about Nat? Oh yes, that half the Territory knew and admired him for helping to make Antelope a place for decent folks.

"Dear God, what if I hadn't come?" Adam barely whispered. Hardwick might be sound asleep but a rancher who lived on guard against two- and four-legged varmints would certainly be a light sleeper.

"Good thing I run onto you, like I did." Hardwick drawled, the next day. "It's a lot of rugged miles between Rock Springs and Antelope." He eyed Adam's strong body. "Can you ride?"

"If you'd asked me that six months ago, I'd have said no." The young doctor laughed. "I can now, though. I've been in West Virginia where they have some great horses."

"No better than our cowponies, I'll wager." Hardwick jealously defended his own. "They might be faster but, by jingo, a man needs a horse that's half human and can get him out of trouble when the shootin' begins."

"Is there a lot of shooting?" Adam tensed.

"Tolerable amount. Not so much since your brother came."

The last miles of the long journey raced as Adam continued to learn from the rancher. "I won't be totally ignorant when I get to Antelope," he confided in his new friend, "thanks to you. By the way, why do you call your ranch the Lazy H? I can figure out it's *H* for Hardwick but I wouldn't think you'd have time for laziness."

His companion's shout of laughter drew the interested attention of everyone in the car. "You're right about that, son." Hardwick's eyes twinkled. "It's just a name. See this?" He drew in the dust that had collected on the windowsill. "We have to brand our cattle and the lazy part just means the H is layin' down on its side. See?" He pointed at his lazy "H"(⊥).

Adam solemnly regarded the little figure. He sighed. "I have a lot more to learn, I guess."

Hardwick sobered. "Adam, any man who's willin' to admit he don't know it all is a jump ahead of the game. Just do your doctrin', keep your ears and eyes open and your mouth closed, and you'll do fine.

"Say, do you have a gal back East?"

Adam couldn't keep from squirming. "Well, not really. I mean, I met a girl, that is, two girls this summer."

"They ain't keen on the West?"

Adam felt Hardwick could see right through him. "One sure isn't." He shifted position again.

"And the other?"

Adam felt his lips curve up into a smile. "If she weren't a well brought up young woman, I think she'd —" He broke off and stared out the window across the aisle over Hardwick's shoulder. *"Look!"*

Hardwick whipped around and unconsciously grabbed for the Colt sixshooters he had earlier showed Adam. With a motion so fast the fascinated doctor could scarcely follow it, the guns were out of their holsters and into his hands. Hardwick's gaze never left the band of Indians on horseback that stood statuelike watching the train.

"Are — are they friendly?"

Hardwick muttered something under his breath and slowly sheathed the sixshooters as the color came back to his face. "Friendly? No. Peaceable? Maybe."

"Do they bother your ranch?"

Hardwick shrugged. "Now and then a steer's missin' and all we find is the hooves. Can't say if it's hungry braves or someone else." His lips tightened into a grim line.

"Do you — I mean, it's hard back East to get any kind of picture of what the situation out here really is." Adam waited, sensing more beneath Hardwick's actions than stolen steers.

For a long time the rancher didn't answer. "There's right and wrong on both sides. I saw what was left of a wagon train after the Indians hit it. Then I saw an Indian camp after a cavalry raid." He turned toward Adam, his eyes molten steel. "I don't ever want to see either again and neither do you." He cleared his throat. "You'll ride along with me from Rock Springs to Antelope."

Adam knew the subject had been closed, permanently.

Nothing Adam had seen so far compared with the ride from Rock Springs where they got off the train up through western Wyoming Territory to Antelope. Those hundred miles offered Adam a hundred new experiences and every emotion known to humankind. Humbled, Adam numbly followed in his guide's tracks.

The sheer beauty of autumn in the Wind River Range made Adam speechless: cliffs with narrow trails that clung to their rock sides and broke off sheer into gorges far below that thundered warning in white water; peaks he could only see by craning his neck, especially Wind River Peak, over 13,000 feet high, that dwarfed all else, yet Hardwick said Wyoming Territory had other peaks even higher! How magnificent was God's creation, Adam realized fully for the first time.

Adam lost count of the times they had to ford creeks, streams, and young rivers that roared their way downward. He learned to hold on stonily and let his horse do the work. Now he knew what Hardwick meant when he had observed that this country called for half-human horses to keep riders out of trouble. The beautiful filly the Browns had graciously let him use might do well in her own environment but out here she'd prove useless.

Yet the danger, fear, and restless anticipation of what might come next couldn't dampen Adam's spirits. Never had he appreciated food as he did now. Even his mother's cooking paled before the hearty fare served on tin plate after being cooked over the open campfires. The rancher never praised Adam for starting campfires but Adam saw growing friendship and respect to match his own and treasured this rare opportunity.

Sleeping on pine needles with nothing between him but a million blazing stars brought rest beyond belief. Not even in medical school where he had cherished sleep had Adam slept so well as on the ground with smoky blankets to keep off the frost that formed every morning.

They heard Antelope before they saw it.

Tinny piano music and the yells of cow-hands and miners in town for Saturday night reached Hardwick and Adam when they dropped down the last fairly steep incline from the forest to a fairly level area below. "Antelope at its noisiest and worst," Hardwick warned. Only the thought that Nat had a long way to go to provide a better place for families dampened Adam's raging enthusiasm.

They swung around a bend. Antelope lay ahead a few hundred yards. Etched into Adam's brain were a few neat, peeling log cabins flanked by hastily thrown together buildings. Dirty tents were on one side and saloons bordered each end of town, the Pronghorn and the Silver. Adam shuddered, yet he only had to lift his eyes to the hills: Like wasted tea leaves that lay in the bottom of an exquisite teacup, such was the contrast between Satan's meddling and God's handiwork. *No wonder Nat pleaded for help,* Adam thought.

Adam squared his shoulders and silently rode forward. On closer inspection he saw a blacksmith shop, a dressmaker's business, and a sprawling building that Hardwick explained held everything from food and clothes to trapping equipment. The main street, if such a dusty thoroughfare could so be called, looked three times wider than any street in Massachusetts and held horses and riders, a lone buckboard, and half a hundred shouting men.

"What's happening?" Adam raised in his stirrups to see better.

The yelling stopped and the roughly dressed men spilled to each side of the street.

"We'd better go back and head for your brother's," Hardwick suggested, as he neck-reined his horse to the right.

The sound of a shot — and a cry from the crowd — stopped Adam from following. What impulse led him to spur his horse on down the street he could not explain. A man loomed in the dust, his feet apart and steady. He still held a Colt in his right hand. Another man lay face down in the road, his fingers still clutching his six-shooter. Although Adam saw a ray of sun glint from the silver star on the erect man's chest, he ignored it and flung himself down beside the fallen cowboy. "Bring a light," he ordered in the same way that kept his assistants in surgery hopping.

"Here, who are you?" the sheriff bellowed. He strode to Adam, gripped his shoulder, and rocked him back on his heels.

With a mighty effort, Adam threw off the

restraining hand. "Get me a light," he repeated, his voice razor-sharp, as he slipped his hand under the wounded man's body. "Good. Bullet went clean through. He's alive but needs surgery. Where's that light?"

"Right here." Hardwick shouldered the sheriff aside and held out a lighted lantern he'd evidently snatched from someone.

"I want to know who you are and what business this is of yours," the sheriff demanded at the top of his lungs.

Adam glanced up only long enough to see a slow smile spread across Hardwick's face. In the dusk outside the circle of lantern light, Hardwick cleared his throat.

"Folks, meet Adam Birchfield, brother of Nat and our new doctor."

Adam ignored the silence followed by a cheer. "I want three strong men — Hardwick, Sheriff, and you." He pointed to a burly man standing nearby. "Where can I take this man to treat him?"

No one answered or moved.

"Confound you all, if I don't get him sutured he's going to die." Adam faced the crowd. "Take him to Nat's."

"The range is better off without Mark Justice," the sheriff grumbled, but he subsided when Adam threw him a fiery glance of scorn.

Each holding a leg or arm, the quartet carried the young cowboy who didn't look over twenty away from the main street to a new-looking peeled log cabin. Too concerned over his first patient in this violent land to pay attention to anyone else, Adam vaguely heard Hardwick say, "Preacher must not be home. No light."

"Then make one," Adam ordered when they got inside and had laid the cowboy on a bright, blanket-covered bed. "This boy's lost a lot of blood." A half-hour later Adam turned from his task. Not a word had been spoken while he cleansed, stitched, and bandaged the gaping hole.

"I oughta take him to jail," the sheriff blustered, but a reluctant smile erased some of his truculence. "Guess it ain't necessary. You'll be responsible for him, Doc?"

"Of course. What did he do, anyway?" Adam's voice struggled to sound matter of fact.

"Got drunk, lost at cards, shot up the Pronghorn, and pulled his gun on me when I tried to arrest him. I had no choice but to shoot —"

"What are you doing in my cabin?" An icy voice asked.

Adam pushed through the others toward the door. "Nat, I'm here!"

68

"Adam?" Strong arms caught him and that single moment of reunion with his beloved brother more than made up for everything that had gone before.

FIVE

Dr. Adam Birchfield's first month in Antelope brought more and different kinds of cases than he had seen during his entire Concord practice. "Did they all save things up until I got here?" he demanded of Nat one evening after wearily finishing up with his last patient.

Nat lifted black eyebrows so like Adam's. His younger brother noted with satisfaction that Nat looked years younger than the fateful night he burst into his cabin to discover it had been turned into a temporary surgery. "Now how could Mrs. Fenner have saved up falling out of a tree until you came?" he teased.

"With no doctor in town, she probably was scared to climb the tree until I got here." Adam stretched his muscles and rejoiced in his newfound strength, the result of riding out to folks who couldn't come in for his help. "And Mrs. Trevor obviously

70

wasn't due to have Junior earlier." He yawned. "Seriously, Nat, what did people do here with no medical help? I know you did what you could. . . ."

"But patching up heads after fights isn't operating on Mrs. Hardwick and having her appendix burst just after you removed it."

Adam shuddered. That particular situation had been a nightmare. Bound by friendship to the first person in Antelope who had welcomed him, it had taken intense prayer, a steady hand, and all his concentration and skill to save Mrs. Hardwick. "A few minutes more and it would have burst inside her and shot poison through her system. Little chance of saving her if that happened. Thank God it didn't."

Nat rose, ruffled his brother's hair the way he did when they were small, and gruffly said, "Your being here means everything on earth to me." He cleared his throat and Adam saw the convulsive motion when he swallowed. "I know it's way too early for you to make any kind of permanent decision, but I'd be the happiest person alive if you decided to stay."

Before Adam could answer he swung out the door of the extra room willing hands had built for "the new Doc." Long and low, partitions divided it into a small waiting area, a work area, and a tiny bedroom with a bunk for Adam. The smell of freshly peeled logs bore witness to the friendship and appreciation of the rugged families served by both Adam and Nat. Although the saloonkeepers and gamblers never came to the small church, they had been generous with money and labor in adding on to the preacher's cabin.

"I wonder what Miss Ivy Ann Brown would think of my new home," Adam said to himself as he headed for his bedroom to wash up before supper. "Or Laurel. They couldn't fault the town's friendliness. It matches what I received from them."

The thought recurred an hour later. Nat sat preparing his next sermon, deep in thought and Scripture. Adam idly flipped through an old medical journal. Suddenly he said, "I'll do it."

"Do what?" Nat raised his dark head. A few silver threads glistened in the lamplight.

"Write to the Browns." Adam searched out the necessary materials. Yet Nat had gone back to his sermon long before Adam collected his thoughts. He hesitated then plunged right into his adventures since leaving Shawnee. He neither overstated nor downplayed the crudity and lawless element but he also included the good done by such solid citizens as Nat, the Hardwicks, and others.

At first encounter I thought the sheriff worse than the so-called outlaws. However, after experiencing a few more Saturday nights in Antelope I understand a lot better. It takes strong persons to build this country. In the past month I have dealt with men who were thrown by horses, clawed by mountain lions, and gored by mean steers. One boy not yet in his teens suffered a broken leg from trying to tame a mustang, a wild horse.

He paused then mischievously added the next paragraph.

I attended a basket social in the brand-new schoolhouse a few nights ago. Imagine buying a basket and finding it stuffed with venison steak instead of fried chicken and containing dried apple tarts in place of apple pie or chocolate cake. The women out here make do with what they have and rely heavily on the country. They have cellars filled with hundreds of jars of home-canned fruit and vegetables. Bushel baskets of potatoes, squash, and other keeping vegetables line cellars dug into the earth. It reminds me of Mother and her pickling and preserving.

Once more he stopped before concluding his thoughts.

It is wild, raw, and uncivilized. Yet a spark of decency has been lit, a small flame ignited and the determination to make Antelope a good place to live burns high. I can't even begin to describe the beauty of this changeable land that smiles with sunshine one day and blusters the next. Snow crowns the nearby mountains already and Nat tells me old-timers say we are due for a hard winter. I suspect my skills will be tested to the utmost. Oh, the rebellious young cowboy is healed and back on the range a wiser person. It amazed me to discover that he holds no bitterness toward the sheriff but feels he got just what he deserved for getting drunk and going crazy, as he describes it. He's so grateful to me that he even came to church the one weekend he could get in from his duties. Nat nearly forgot his sermon when he saw the boy come in.

I believe even more firmly than ever that if, no, when, Antelope gets enough godly people such incidents will dwindle and fade away. God grant that more pioneers and less of the lower element will choose to come West.

Respectfully yours,
Adam Birchfield, M.D.

Let Miss Ivy Ann and her family shiver and exclaim over this. Would his letter be a seed, planted and waiting for the right climate to make it grow? The Bible story of the sower came to mind as Nat had told it the week before. Adam adapted it to the Brown family, using what knowledge he had gained while there.

The seed that fell by the wayside to be eaten by fowl could represent Ivy Ann. He suspected she'd be easily distracted from serious things and let the most precious ones be taken away without ever realizing it.

Perhaps the seed would sprout with Laurel or Thomas, maybe even Sadie. But could it withstand stony places such as the Wyoming Territory must appear to them? Or scorching heat and thorns that represented leaving all they knew for the unknown?

Adam sighed. Not many places could offer the rich soil from which pioneers and explorers sprang a hundredfold as the seed in the thirteenth chapter of Matthew did. He stretched and stared at Nat's bent head.

A rush of love that had been planted in childhood and carefully nurtured through all the years now bloomed stronger than ever. Good old Nat, preaching and visiting, never too busy to lend a hand raising a cabin for a new family or too weary to answer a call in the middle of the night along with Adam when a crisis came! Heroes in history and storybooks dimmed alongside Nat, and Adam felt that every day in his company wound more invisible chains to keep the brothers together in Antelope for a lifetime. *What would Father say? And Mother, whose aching heart longed for her sons?* Yet in the past days a great tumult in his heart warned Adam such might well be his fate, his call, his service.

He bade Nat goodnight and sought sleep in his own room. The next day his letter began the journey east.

Never could Adam Birchfield have imagined the furor that accompanied the arrival of his letter in West Virginia. Life at Red Cedars had gone on undisturbed, like a quiet pool that stills once the waves from a rock thrown into it subside. Ivy Ann continued charming every male who chanced on her home. Laurel became quieter than ever, often wondering at herself and even more at

Ivy Ann. She couldn't believe how quickly even her fickle twin forgot Adam after going to so much effort to enslave him. "Ivy by name, Ivy by nature," Laurel muttered to herself when the laughing girl clung to the arm of the handsomest man at different gatherings.

The family worked hard harvesting and storing up for winter. Yet Laurel knew restlessness as never before. More often than she cared to admit, she found that her gaze turned west. Once Ivy Ann petulantly demanded, "What's out there?"

Laurel felt streaks of red stain her smooth skin. "A sunset worth watching," she quietly answered, glad for the truth that covered a deeper yearning.

Then The Letter came, forever capitalized in Laurel's mind.

As usual, Ivy Ann snatched it with a cry of joy. Her dark brown eyes sparkled. "Everyone, come! A letter from Adam Birchfield." Her long, pink skirts swayed as she childishly clutched the letter with both hands.

"Well, for land's sake, open it," Sadie commanded. A pleased look settled over her face. "How nice of the young man to write when he must be so busy out there in the West."

Laurel ached to take the letter and read it privately. Above all she resented the way Ivy Ann acted as if it had been written just to her, especially when Laurel saw it had been addressed to Mr. and Mrs. Thomas Brown and family.

"He says things are going well and —" Ivy Ann maddeningly started to put the news in her own words.

"Just read what Dr. Birchfield wrote, daughter." Thomas didn't often issue commands but when he did he expected immediate obedience.

Ivy Ann looked injured but complied, except when she got to the most exciting parts. She then interjected little shivers of mock fright until Laurel wanted to shake her.

"The basket social sounds like fun," Ivy dreamily said when she finished and let the pages drift to the floor.

"Is that all you got out of his letter?" Incredulous, Laurel stared at her sister.

"Why, you don't really believe all that about people being clawed by wild animals, do you?" Ivy's eyes opened wide in consternation. "Surely Adam just put that in to entertain us."

Laurel glanced at her father. He looked skyward then back before sharing a secret grin with her. "Remember what he said before he ever went out there? I don't doubt that every word is true."

"Besides —" Laurel couldn't keep a little malice from her voice. "Adam said he hated and despised deceitfulness above anything else. You must remember that, Ivy Ann."

Her twin turned scarlet. "Oh, that's right." She bent to pick up the pages and looked innocent enough when she straightened. "Imagine him hinting for us to move West. Can you think of anything sillier?"

"I can," Laurel told her, but Ivy Ann just sniffed. Laurel saw the unreadable look that passed between her parents and her heart skipped a beat. Of course they wouldn't think of leaving Red Cedars but the flicker of longing in her father's eyes matched what lay in Laurel's heart. "I wish I were a man. I'd go out there and be part of creating a new land," she burst out.

"You must have stayed out in the sun too long today," Ivy Ann said sweetly and felt Laurel's forehead. "Dear me, what a tempest Adam's letter caused! But then, perhaps he intended it should." She yawned and patted her mouth with her well-cared-for hand. "Oh, I'll answer his letter tomorrow. Poor dear, he's probably starved for companionship with his own kind." She clutched the letter and swept out.

"It would be nice if you also wrote to the young man," Sadie told Laurel.

"Why? Ivy will tell him the news." She tried to keep the bitterness from her voice and deliberately yawned as her twin had done. "Goodnight."

"Goodnight, dear." Their voices followed her up the stairs.

Why should Ivy Ann expect and take all the happiness out of everything, draining it to the last drop and leaving nothing for anyone else? Laurel's love for her twin warred with the deepest indignation she had ever felt. *Why do I care so much? I never did before,* Laurel thought. *Those few looks I shared with Dr. Birchfield are meaningless.* She fell asleep troubled by strange dreams of a greatly changed Adam whose dark eyes glowed with welcome and whose lips whispered words of love Laurel had never heard before.

When she awakened, new resolve filled her. This time she would not allow Ivy Ann to take over. After her sister patted her light brown curls into place and hurried down to breakfast, Laurel made a hasty toilette and read Adam's letter. That afternoon she stole time from other duties to dash off a quick message of thanks and an invitation for

Adam to write "to the family" when he could. Her heart beating rapidly at her unaccustomed daring, Laurel held her tongue when Ivy Ann sat down to write her own letter. When she nonchalantly said she'd put it in an envelope if Ivy liked, she surreptitiously slipped in her own note. The heavens might fall when an answer came but until then Laurel clung to her first show of independence and rejoiced.

Several weeks later a second letter came. Again Adam had addressed it to the family; again Ivy Ann appropriated it as her own and doled out its contents. When she came to the statement, "Thank you so very much for your messages," she frowned. "*Messages?* Why should he say that?"

"You shared more than one piece of news, didn't you?" Laurel stayed cool outside and felt reprieved when the frown faded and Ivy read on. Adam closed with a challenge, evidently in response to something Ivy Ann had written.

Folks like you are still needed. The hunting here is wonderful. Fifty males to every female.

"Whatever is that s'posed to mean?" Ivy Ann peered at the cryptic message. "That there are more female deer?"

"Don't you get it?" Laurel threw back her head and laughed. "With only a few married women and even fewer single young women, the odds are in the females' favor."

"Don't be vulgar." Ivy Ann's face tightened and her eyes flashed. "As if decent young women like us would ever look at anyone in the Wyoming Territory!"

"You did enough looking at Dr. Birchfield when he visited here," Laurel reminded. "And he's in the Wyoming Territory."

Ivy gasped but Thomas backed up Laurel.

"That's right. From what I gather that brother of his is a cultured man as well." His eyes twinkled. "If you run out of beaux here you can always go West, girls."

"I doubt the westerners would have us," Laurel teased, and she felt rewarded when Ivy sat bolt upright.

"I guess I could do anything any old girl in the West could do, if I made up my mind to do it."

"But you never would," Sadie put in, smiling at the flustered girl. "Admit it, Ivy. You like comfort too well."

"You're all picking on me!" Storm clouds gathered in the fair face. "If I didn't love Red Cedars so much, I'd up and go West just to show you how wrong you are."

Laurel buried her face in a small pillow and laughed herself sick. How clever of Adam to needle Ivy Ann so subtly. Now if she could again smuggle a message in her sister's letter. . . .

Christmas came in around of festivities. Spicy evergreen branches turned Red Cedars into a bower. Fruitcake ripened in the pantry. A multitude of gifts arrived from Ivy Ann's followers who vied to win her favor. Fewer came for Laurel but she honestly didn't mind. What gift could compare with the beautiful Indian moccasins Adam had sent the twins? Handmade of soft deerskin, Laurel cherished both the gift and the thoughtfulness behind it.

Ivy Ann scoffed at such a present but her twin noticed how she made a point of displaying the moccasins when her beaux came. "Wasn't it just sweet of Dr. Birchfield to send *me* such an unusual Christmas gift?"

A curiously carved necklace for Sadie accompanied the moccasins as well as a hand-tooled leather belt for Thomas, along with a crude but surprisingly attractive small painting of the area near Antelope. Adam explained in a note that Mrs. Hardwick had done a similar one for him while recuperating from her appendectomy. He'd begged her to paint another and insisted on paying for it so he could send it to the Browns.

Laurel gazed at the rolling, tree-dotted hills that swept upward to solid timber then white peaks and the bluest sky she'd ever seen. The longing within her that had gone dormant from all the hustle and bustle of Christmas came to glowing life. *Someday,* she vowed, *I am going to see it for myself. How or when I don't know. But I will go West — someday.*

On Christmas Eve afternoon Laurel rode into Shawnee for a few last-minute items needed in the cooking of tomorrow's big dinner that would be shared with many friends and neighbors. She got what she needed, kept a sharp lookout toward the cloud-clotted sky, and stumbled when she stepped down from the porch of the store.

"Careful, Miss Brown." One of Ivy Ann's suitors neatly caught Laurel's arm and kept her from falling.

Laurel felt herself redden. "Thanks, James. You saved me from a nasty spill."

"May I present my cousin, Beauregard Worthington?" James stepped aside to let a tall, fair man dressed in the latest fashion come forward. "Beau, this is Miss Laurel Brown. Beau's here from Charleston for the holidays."

"My pleasure, Miss Brown." The strikingly

handsome man bent over her hand as if she were the Queen of England.

"Beau will be coming to dinner with us tomorrow," James rushed on. "When your mother heard he'd be here she graciously included him in the invitation."

Laurel smiled up into the tall stranger's deep blue eyes. She could see her reflection in them, rosy-cheeked from the late afternoon chill, with a few curls escaping from under her bonnet. "You will be more than welcome, Mr. Worthington." She quickly mounted before either of the men could offer assistance. "I must hurry or darkness will overtake me." She smiled again and felt her heart flutter at the unmistakable admiration in the visitor's eyes.

"Until tomorrow, Miss Brown."

"Until tomorrow, Mr. Worthington, James." Her pony swung toward home. *What a handsome man,* Laurel thought. Ivy Ann will — no! she determined. Not this time. *I met him first.*

Six

The twins wore the same gowns for Christmas dinner they had worn for their twentieth birthday party. Ivy Ann complained and begged for a new dress but soon ceased pouting for fear it would leave a wrinkle in her smooth face.

Laurel serenely donned the lovely blue gown and secretly smiled. She had stolen a march on her twin for once by offering to decorate the long table and do the place-cards they no longer bothered with except for very special occasions.

"Who is Beauregard Worthington?" Ivy Ann demanded at her sister's elbow. "And why are you putting him next to you?"

"He's a visiting cousin of James." Laurel forced herself not to betray any kind of interest.

"What a name!" Ivy Ann threw her hands into the air. "What is he, a country bumpkin whose parents gave him a pretentious name he can never live up to?"

"No—o. I met him briefly yesterday at the store. He seemed so appreciative of being included at dinner it seemed right to seat him by one of the family."

"Oh, the shy and humble type." Ivy Ann tossed her head until the curls loosened and surrounded her laughing face. "Leave it to you to be kind to the misfits."

Laurel smothered a laugh and quickly diverted her twin. "I put James on one side of you. Do you want Stephen or Phillip on the other side?"

Ivy cocked her head to one side and a calculating look crept into her eyes. "Well, I like Stephen better, but Phillip sent me the nicest present so I guess I owe it to him." Beauregard Worthington passed out of her consciousness, at least for the moment.

Laurel made sure she got downstairs before Ivy and instead of making a grand entrance she met James, his family, and their guest at the door. The same admiration that had shone in Beauregard's eyes the day before had deepened significantly. "Miss Brown, how charming you look!" He bowed over her hand, his immaculate clothing winning her approval. A little stir behind them made Laurel and her guest turn. She noticed he kept her hand in his.

"Why — who's that?" The blond man looked from blue-clad Laurel to the pink-gowned Ivy Ann.

"James, didn't you tell your cousin there are two of us?" Ivy tapped his shoulder with her furled fan. But the look she sent Laurel promised all kinds of dire things in retaliation. "You *are* Beauregard Worthington, aren't you?"

Under cover of the flowing conversation a bit later Ivy Ann managed to furiously whisper, "Why didn't you tell me the best-looking man that's been in this part of West Virginia for ages would be having dinner with us?"

Laurel opened her eyes wide in false innocence. "That shy, humble bumpkin with the pretentious name? Why ever would you want to hear about him?"

"You'll be sorry."

Laurel just laughed at the childish threat and smugly led Beauregard in to dinner. From where they sat, they could barely glimpse Ivy Ann between her devoted swains. At least until the feast ended she'd have no opportunity to carry out any scheme.

Laurel felt her heart pitty-pat in the way she associated with heroines in the few romance novels she had read. *Why not use the time to make an impression on this well-mannered, interesting man?*

Before the end of dinner, she learned that Beauregard not only was her senior by ten years but was deeply involved in politics, loved riding, and intended to someday run for governor of the state. Unfortunately, his deep voice attracted attention and the rest of the family and guests also gleaned the same information. Ivy Ann's avid listening warned Laurel that her twin considered Beauregard Worthington not only the best-looking man around, but the best catch as well. Yet even when the more vivacious twin, Stephen, Phillip, and a few other young men and women joined Laurel and Beau, Beau continued his discussion with Laurel, whose intelligent questions spurred him to share his ideas and aspirations.

At a disadvantage, Ivy Ann finally broke up the conversation by almost forcing the merry crowd to join in singing Christmas carols. Laurel grinned at the ploy. Ivy Ann knew how white and dainty her hands looked when she played the spinet. Flushed from the warm room and attention, Ivy had never been more beautiful.

To Laurel's delight and Ivy Ann's obvious chagrin, Beau merely thanked the musician for her playing when he left but lingered with Laurel. "Miss Brown, may I call tomorrow? I'd like to finish our discussion."

"Of course," said Laurel triumphantly as she closed the door.

Her triumph faded, however, before the blaze in Ivy Ann's eyes and the tight line of her mouth. Ivy didn't dare say anything in front of their parents but once upstairs she turned on Laurel.

"Just what do you think you're doing, hogging Beauregard Worthington all evening?"

Laurel could have laughed it off; she knew in her heart she should. God did not want families to quarrel. Yet the sore spot formed in childhood when everyone petted and praised her twin had been intensified over Adam Birchfield and irritated further by her own growing dissatisfaction of living in her sister's shadow. The taste of victory lay sweet in her mouth. "Isn't it about time?"

Ivy Ann's eyelids half-closed in the danger signal Laurel well knew and usually heeded. "What do you mean?"

Laurel walked to the dressing table, seated herself, and deliberately let down her curls. Ivy's flushed, angry image stared at her over her shoulder. Suddenly Laurel had borne enough. She turned and faced her sister. "Ever since we were big enough to toddle you've had to be first. Pretty, popular Ivy

Ann. Quiet Laurel, following a few steps behind. It has never mattered which of us found a new friend or beau. Always they've eventually turned from me to you, Ivy Ann. How many boys that I could have cared for did you deliberately take away, even when they meant nothing to you?"

Ivy's face turned to pearl but she didn't answer.

Laurel felt exhausted. "I love you more than anything or anyone except God. But it isn't right and it isn't good for *either* of us to continue the way we have. You need to learn that you can't have everything you demand in life."

"Meaning Beauregard Worthington?" A small smile crept over Ivy's face until she looked like a sleepy kitten. Yet Laurel knew how sharp her claws could be.

She sighed and didn't back down. "If he chooses to call on me, I am going to welcome him and enjoy his company." She carefully removed her blue dress and hung it away, noting her twin's unusual silence. But when Laurel pulled her nightgown over her head she caught Ivy Ann's whispered response.

"We'll just see about that."

Was it worth it? Had staging a tiny revolution done anything except challenge Ivy to do her best — or worst — and capture Beau's interest? *Dear God,* Laurel silently prayed, *maybe You created me to be the giver. But how can Ivy Ann ever become a woman if she takes and takes and takes? Or am I just excusing my own selfishness?* Troubled, she fell asleep without an answer.

If Thomas and Sadie Brown hadn't been so involved with the never-ending duties of Red Cedars, they would have noticed the latest romantic triangle. A hundred times before, Ivy Ann had charmed the young men who called on Laurel as well as on herself. But this time Laurel didn't meekly step aside. Deep in her innermost being she knew she cared little for Beauregard Worthington in spite of his eligible qualities. But the same flame of independence that had brought about the most serious argument the twins ever had steadied into resolve. What she had said in a moment of truth bore heavily on her mind. Going on as she had, giving in to her twin, set a silent approval to Ivy's idea she could and would be first in everything and with everyone.

No more, Laurel promised herself. And yet the new coldness Ivy bestowed on her almost shattered Laurel's stance. Childhood arguments and quarrels, conducted without their parents' knowledge, had always ended with the girls making up before bedtime in compliance with their Bible teachings. This latest rift did not and, for the first time in her life, Laurel refused to apologize for the disagreement and take the blame as she had done before.

"Dear God," she prayed one night when Ivy Ann had fallen asleep without even a goodnight, "your Son taught that blessed are the meek. Does meek mean being a doormat all my life? I don't think so." She remembered what their minister said in his last sermon concerning the Beatitudes.

"Moses is identified as a meek man. Can we picture him groveling or effacing himself to the point of losing his personality? No. When we study different languages from Bible times we learn that meek means *teachable,* not docile and spiritless as people now call it."

Ivy Ann's frosty treatment of Laurel in private matched the January winds that blew across Red Cedars and Shawnee. When others were present, Ivy clung prettily to her sister as usual. Beau extended his visits and often rode out in spite of the snow. Cutters called for the twins and sleighing parties that ended at neighbors' homes or back at Red Cedars for spiced cider or foamy chocolate brightened the twins' winter. Beau automatically took his place by Laurel and her natural vanity and pride swelled. Yet devious Ivy managed to sit on Beau's other side an amazing number of times. Laurel smiled to herself. Her pretty twin seized every opportunity, and prepared for them. A half-dozen times Laurel found her reading and discussing events of the day with their father. Before Beau appeared, such talk had left her bored and restless.

Wise Ivy Ann! Her knowledge of subjects that interested Beau never went deep, but a few well-chosen comments could keep the intelligent and dedicated young man talking for hours.

"I didn't think at first that your sister cared about anything but parties and dresses and flirting," he candidly told Laurel one evening while they waited for Ivy to come downstairs. "A person shouldn't go by first impressions, should they?"

" 'Man looketh on the outward appearance, but the Lord looketh on the heart.' "[*] Laurel couldn't help quoting, thinking of Ivy's deceitful mind.

"Shakespeare certainly had a way of getting to the core of things, didn't he?" Beau

[*]1 Samuel 16:7 (KJV)

said enthusiastically.

Laurel didn't have the heart to tell him the quote came from the Bible. Neither did she have time. Ivy Ann ran lightly downstairs in spite of her heavy cloak and shoes and warm gloves.

"Ready?" Her cheeks shone against the dark cloak.

Laurel sighed inwardly. The look in Beau's eyes betrayed the beginning of the end. At least he had made a good fight, far better than any young man before him. Laurel felt like tearing off her own heavy clothing and refusing to join the party calling from the sleighs gathered outside. An hour later she wished she had instead of silently submitting to Beau's hand under her elbow. Ivy's adoring gaze shone clear even in the starlight. Her upturned face and expression of deep interest sickened her twin. The chances of Ivy caring about anything political equaled those that the world would end before they reached home.

Yet, Laurel considered, *perhaps Ivy Ann did care.* If she captured Beau, she might one day live in the governor's mansion! Laurel let her lips curl into a reluctant smile. No woman of her acquaintance could better carry such a position. Ivy's charm would dazzle even opponents and prove a real asset to a young man on the rise to fame.

So could you, a reminding voice whispered.

She shook her head. The last thing she wanted would be the endless round of gaiety, soirées, and excitement that delighted her twin. An unbidden vision of a tall, dark man etched against a scene similar to the painting by Mrs. Hardwick shot into her mind. She longed to hear his impassioned voice sharing the conviction that God wanted him to go West.

She compared the two young men who had most touched her life. Beau — equally dedicated, but toward a profession that would bring glory as well as service. Adam — who turned his back on a lucrative practice and future, crossed swords with his father, and followed the dream in his heart to a rough but needy town thousands of miles from home.

Laurel felt herself tottering on the edge of an important and enlarged understanding. Not until the evening ended with Ivy twitting her about letting her mind wander did Laurel realize a startling truth: Every trace of annoyance with her sister's flirting had vanished. How trite, how unworthy to care when men and a few courageous women and children struggled to create a home in the wilderness!

Like a stranger in an unfamiliar land, Laurel observed the pretty young women vying for attention with Ivy Ann in the center. Even a few pitying glances aimed at Laurel when Beau hovered near her twin failed to penetrate the new armor she wore.

I feel as if tonight I have put away childish things and become a woman while they are still playing with dolls. Laurel smiled at the thought and continued watching her friends. Had Sally-Ellen always simpered so? Strange that she hadn't noticed how James brayed when he laughed, usually at the wrong times. One by one she considered those she had known for years and those who had entered her life later. She mentally measured them against Adam Birchfield and found them lacking. Only the older men, those who had fought and come home with too-wise eyes to razed homes and the need to start again, could meet Laurel's high standards.

Because of her experience, Laurel only smiled tolerantly when Ivy Ann triumphantly confronted her the next morning. "Beau is coming to see *me* today."

"That's nice," Laurel said absently. She poked up the fire until it roared into the time-blackened chimney.

"Don't you care?" Ivy Ann looked totally astounded. Her mouth dropped open in an unbecoming pose.

"Should I?" Laurel raised her eyebrows.

"But he's been coming to see you!" Ivy Ann petulantly flounced onto a chair across from her sister.

Laurel instantly caught her twin's mood. Half the joy Ivy Ann received from Beau's asking to call on her had been drowned by the fact her twin simply didn't care! Laurel threw her head back and laughed, a clear, ringing laugh that dispelled any idea Beauregard Worthington's transfer of affections would give her a moment's thought.

Ivy sullenly stared and, when Laurel settled down and put her feet toward the warm fire, she never let her gaze wander.

"Ivy Ann, do you really care for Beau or is all the excitement just to take him away from another woman?"

Ivy's eyes glittered. "He's nice. He's going to be someone. The woman he marries will have beautiful clothes, live in a home with servants, and be adored and cared for."

"Petted."

An angry flush marred the other's face. "Why don't you admit it's sour grapes, Laurel? I've got him if I want him and you're jealous." She held to her crumbling position with clenched fists.

"You don't believe that." Laurel knew she'd hit home by the way Ivy flinched and the way her color deepened. "Do you really think all the things you mentioned will make you happy? What about when children come and you're at home while Beau has to attend the parties for the sake of his office? What then, Ivy Ann? Or suppose he's terribly ill. Will you care for him gladly?"

Her sister's lips quivered like a butterfly poised for flight. "You're perfectly horrid to bring up all those things, Mountain Laurel Brown!"

Laurel felt a hundred years older than Ivy Ann. She rose and put her arm around Ivy's shoulder. "Mama and Daddy have taught us marriage is from God and unless we love our husbands with all our hearts — next to God Himself — we must never enter into it."

Ivy's slim shoulders stiffened and Laurel squeezed them. "I won't say more but never forget that once we say 'I do' only death can cancel that promise before God." She left Ivy staring into the fire, silenced for once.

For a few weeks Beau shamefacedly sought out Laurel at times and talked with her as before. Yet all Ivy had to do was enter the room to claim his attention. Laurel discovered how sorry she felt for the young man. No boy to be teased, but a man to be reckoned with. Couldn't Ivy Ann realize her flirtatious ways wouldn't be tolerated forever?

Thomas Brown spoke out at dinner one evening when only the four gathered for the meal. He rested his forearms on the table after the blessing. "Is young Worthington courting you, Laurel, or Ivy Ann?" He scowled. "I don't like the tittle-tattle in Shawnee about one man and twin girls."

"Daddy!" Ivy Ann sounded horrified but Laurel caught a satisfied gleam in her dark brown eyes that went so well with a favorite pink dress. "Do you really think Beau would come courting us both at once?"

"Beau and I are good friends and always have been," Laurel quietly said. "As far as courting —" Her eloquent shrug said how little it mattered.

Yet all her lack of caring and common sense couldn't prevent shock spreading through her a few nights later when she discovered Beau and Ivy Ann kissing in a way no girl should allow unless she were betrothed.

When Ivy Ann pulled away with a trill of laughter and caroled, "To think I thought you liked Laurel best," righteous indignation rose to new heights in Laurel. She would break free from her twin, no matter how far she must go.

SEVEN

Now that Laurel Brown had bit in her teeth, she prepared herself to run with the speed of a fine West Virginia racehorse. Item by item she smuggled into a large trunk: dresses; bonnets; plain things for the most part. She could work slowly for not until spring would she dare attempt the long journey West. In the dark night hours while Ivy Ann slept and murmured in pleasant dreams, Laurel collected things that wouldn't be missed and spread her other clothing wide to hide the gaps. She hated the secrecy. With all her heart she longed to go to her parents and say, "This is something I have to do."

But she could not. They would forbid her to embark on such a mad escapade worthy of Ivy Ann and not her dependable self. She knew she would never go against their expressed command.

Now that she no longer paid attention to

Beau, some of Ivy's interest flagged but she hid it well. Laurel suspected pride kept her from discarding him too soon. Besides, his promising future continued to intrigue Ivy. Until she met another and brighter star she found it desirable to stay high in Beau's esteem.

Laurel avoided any confrontations with her twin but, inevitably, Ivy Ann provoked her beyond endurance. The pretty blue dress remained Laurel's best and she saved it for special occasions only. Once or twice Ivy had asked permission to wear it and was refused. Laurel knew how careless Ivy was with clothing. The pink birthday dress already had a tiny tear in the hem, invisibly mended by Laurel but a reminder of Ivy's irresponsible attitude.

That same forget-me-not dress laid claim to Laurel's affections for another reason as well. She had seen Adam Birchfield's admiring glance when she wore it. When she got to Antelope, Laurel intended to wear that gown the first time she saw Adam.

Spring came early and Laurel rejoiced. Ivy Ann flitted between Beau and others. The one afternoon Laurel returned from an invigorating ride that tossed her light brown hair and left her cheeks rosy. She burst into the parlor calling, "Ivy Ann! You should have come, it's just grand out."

A girl in a forget-me-not blue dress guilt-ily leaped to her feet. The china cup she held tilted and a stream of raspberry cordial cascaded down the soft folds of the dress.

"Ivy, how could you?" Laurel grabbed her twin's shoulders and marched her toward the stairs, ignoring the startled protest from her cowed but defiant twin. This time Ivy Ann would not escape justice. Sadie had stepped into the hall, back early from an er-rand in town. She followed the twins up-stairs, scolding all the way.

"Did you have permission to wear Laurel's dress?" she snapped. None of her usual ami-ability softened her features.

"N—no." Ivy Ann looked six instead of twenty. Mama's wrath knew few bounds once provoked.

"The dress is ruined," Laurel cried, her anger turned to numbness while Mama helped get the blue dress off Ivy.

Mama's mouth buttoned itself shut. "This isn't the last of this, girls. There's company downstairs and you're to go back and apologize to Mr. Worthington for this scene," she finally ordered Ivy Ann. "Laurel, I need help in the kitchen."

"I can't go down." Ivy Ann shivered. "Beau will — won't —"

"I expect you dressed and downstairs in five minutes." Mama snatched a simple gray dress from the wardrobe. "Wear this."

Obviously frightened, Ivy Ann got into the dress, smoothed her hair, and followed Mama. Laurel held out the wide skirt panels and wondered if the front breadth could be removed.

"Why bother?" She wadded up the gown and threw it into a heap in the corner. "I'll never wear the spoiled thing again, anyway. Not after it's been ruined and made over." The numbness passed and an exultant wave of gladness filled her. In a short time she'd be gone. Never again could Ivy Ann selfishly take and ruin what rightfully belonged to her.

Beau didn't stay long and the girls avoided each other's company until supper. Afterward Thomas gathered Sadie and the twins into the parlor. "Ivy Ann, you have acted abominably and I'm ashamed of you."

Laurel couldn't help but feel a little sorry for the drooping figure huddled in a chair that heightened her deceptively frail figure. *If Daddy ever boomed at her like that!*

"Go get the blue dress," Thomas commanded Ivy Ann. "Laurel, bring down the pink birthday dress."

She started to protest but saw the stony

look in her father's face and did what she'd been told, following a thoroughly subdued Ivy Ann. Back in the parlor Thomas spread the stained gown out over his knees.

"Sadie, will the stain come out?"

"I don't know." She looked at the ruined gown. "It spread so far. We'll probably have to take out a panel and make it straighter but it won't be as pretty." She sent a sympathizing glance toward Laurel.

Thomas took the frothy pink gown in his big hands, careful not to let their roughness mar the delicate material. "Laurel, this dress is yours from now on. Ivy Ann will wear the blue until it is worn out, once it's been fixed."

Mutiny sprang to Ivy's face and protest caught in Laurel's throat. Before either could speak, Thomas spoke in the voice he reserved for only the most portentous times. "The matter is settled and *no one* is to say another word about it. Laurel, put the pink dress away. Ivy, put the blue gown to soak or whatever it needs."

Ivy Ann stumbled out, her eyes glazed with tears. Laurel took her new pink gown upstairs and reluctantly stowed it in the big trunk destined for Antelope. *Could she ever wear it without remembering this awful day?* She must. She had no other beautiful gown, just simple clothing and outgrown dresses.

The power of Thomas Brown's ultimatum had an effect on both twins. Neither mentioned the dress but it hung between them like a gauzy curtain of misunderstanding and resentment. Laurel wearily counted the days until she could slip away. She watched and waited until one afternoon both parents and Ivy Ann were absent from Red Cedars. Then she hurriedly arranged for her trunk to be taken to the railway station and shipped west. If her calculations proved right, it should reach Antelope just before she arrived.

Now every day became bittersweet. Saying goodbye to the horses and rolling hills and mountains brought pain. So did the gnawing knowledge of her deception. She had sworn to secrecy the old friend who picked up her trunk and shipped it. Nothing remained except a few days that stretched like an eternity in her heart.

In the closing chapter of her life at Red Cedars, Laurel often wondered if she should forget the whole thing, confess her sins to her parents, and have her father retrieve her trunk.

The sight of Ivy Ann as blithe and selfish as ever hardened Laurel's plans. "It isn't like it's forever," she mumbled to a swaying laurel clump already showing signs of swelling buds. "Someday I'll come back." She firmly refused to examine Adam's possible reaction to a madcap young woman who ran away from home and traveled West unchaperoned. Time enough to consider that on the train journey that loomed like forbidden fruit.

Before sunup that fateful spring morning Laurel's tears fell on the carefully written notes she placed on the tall chest of drawers. After tying the strings of her plainest dark bonnet, Laurel walked the miles to Shawnee and began her journey. She kept her head down so the few curious passengers wouldn't ask where she was going so early on a midweek workday. Once on her way, no one would know or heed her, she thought, never realizing that her lovely eyes and wellbred manner would attract attention all the way from home to the Wyoming Territory.

Laurel hadn't known what a mess of contradictions she was until she left Red Cedars and headed West. At times her heart quailed and she fought the desire to get off at every stop. Yet part of her exulted at her new freedom, and a fierce pride in breaking away from Ivy Ann sustained her. Months earlier Adam Birchfield had opened wide his dark eyes at the changing country. Now Laurel Brown gasped and frankly stared. How ignorant she had been of anything outside her own county, her own state, her own little world!

How many rivers did they cross? How many miles of free swaying grass? How many spring freshets and sunny days gave way to the relentless *clack-clack* of the wheels? How many small children did she wave to, barefooted, gap-toothed urchins whose longing for adventure clearly showed on freckled faces that watched the train out of sight? Each time Laurel hugged close to her heart that she actually was on this adventure. Once she secretly pinched herself to make sure it wasn't all a dream. Then she laughed until those around her gazed at the fresh face set off by the plain dark bonnet and traveling gown.

Cramped at times and wishing for a bath, nothing daunted Laurel for long. When she grew irritated at the lack of all the comforts she had taken for granted at home, she privately reminded herself how lucky she was, as Adam had said, to be riding a snorting iron horse all those miles instead of following in the dust of a creaking wagon.

Her first sight of the distant Rockies left her speechless. Never had she felt as insignificant as the moment her gaze beheld the jutting peaks that looked determined to pierce the bottom of heaven. Mountain after snowy mountain loomed until at last she heard the charmed call: "Rock Springs!"

She had done it.

Stiff from the long and tiring journey, Laurel stepped into a world she wouldn't have believed existed. A world of bellowing cattle being driven in for shipping, of dusty men in boots with impossibly tall heels, of curses and the jangle of spurs.

Suddenly her joy faded. Why hadn't she thought things through better? *How on earth could she get from Rock Springs to Antelope?* She grabbed her dwindling courage in both hands as she timidly queried a fellow passenger. "Where is the stage to Antelope?"

His open face showed astonishment. "Stage? There ain't no such thing, miss."

"Well, people go there. How?"

He scratched his head. "Blamed if I know. I never lost anything in Antelope so I never wondered."

Laurel wanted to scream with laughter. If Ivy Ann could see this friendly but simple fellow she'd absolutely die.

She wasn't Ivy Ann, so she'd best start wondering even if this man never had. Yet no one seemed to be able to help until a slender young man whose spotless linen and grooming made him stand out like sunflowers in a violet patch strode toward her. His high heels gave him the appearance of height but Laurel guessed him to be only a few inches taller than her own five foot six inches. Blond, cleanshaven, and thoroughly dapper, he could have stepped into any West Virginia home.

"Miss, did I hear you say you needed to go to Antelope?" Curiosity lit his glowing amber eyes.

For a second Laurel recoiled. Those eyes reminded her of the eyes of a tiger she once saw in a book — wild and dangerous. She hesitated.

"The reason I ask is that a crude wagon road has been built to haul in supplies. I'm taking a wagonload in tomorrow morning. A couple of men are going with me and one woman."

Laurel's joy knew no bounds. "A woman?"

The man smiled. "She's not exactly your type, but she's goodhearted. Storekeeper's wife. She came out for a burying."

Relief washed through the tired girl. "Where can I find her?"

"Boardinghouse." The man jerked a tanned finger with its scrupulously clean nail down the street. "You can stay there

111

overnight. One thing —"

Her heart pounded. *What now?*

"It's a real bumpy ride." White teeth gleamed in his sun-warmed face. "Where's your baggage?" He glanced at the reticule she carried.

"I sent a trunk ahead."

"Must be the one the agent said was bound for Antelope. I'll see to it. It's been here a few days but we don't rightly have a schedule into Antelope. By the way, I'm Dan Sharpe."

She didn't offer her hand but she smiled. "I'm Miss Brown." Five minutes later she followed her self-appointed protector into the parlor of a boardinghouse.

"Mrs. Greer, meet Miss Brown. She's going to Antelope with us tomorrow."

The double-chinned face dropped in surprise but Mrs. Greer snapped it shut and quickly smiled. "Why, nice to meet you!" Her eyes almost closed when she smiled. Laurel appreciated the way she obviously refrained from asking why a young woman from the East would be headed toward Antelope. Instead she merely chatted after Laurel paid for her supper, breakfast, and night's lodging. She told the girl they had about a hundred miles of the wildest Wyoming country ever to travel. They would put up at ranches that welcomed the chance to buy fresh supplies and get outside news. *Mama would approve of Mrs. Greer,* Laurel thought.

At last the good woman ran down. Laurel felt she must explain at least a little. "Doctor Birchfield visited our family in West Virginia," she said. Her heart pounded in her ears. "He said Antelope needed Christian women and families and that his brother was making it a place for decent people to live."

"Land sakes!" The moon face opposite her positively glowed. "Are you Dr. Birchfield's young lady? Why, Miss Brown, he and that brother of his are doing more to bring common decency to Antelope than you can ever imagine." She rushed on and mercifully spared Laurel from having to answer her question.

Dan Sharpe's promise proved true. Much of the misnamed road to Antelope jolted Laurel until her bones ached. Mrs. Greer laughed her cushiony laugh and told the weary girl, "You need more padding, like me."

All Laurel could do was grin feebly and hang on. When they came to places laboriously widened to accommodate the supply wagon, she gritted her teeth, closed her eyes against the canyons that plunged on both sides of them, and prayed. Only once did her sense of humor break through her misery. When Mrs. Greer cheerfully boasted how fine it was to have a road instead of having to ride horseback the whole way or be born in Antelope to get there, Laurel secretly wondered if she'd ever have the courage to leave it once she got there.

"We're going to make this into a real road one of these days," Dan Sharpe promised and lifted a tawny eyebrow. Again Laurel thought of that tiger. She sensed that like his feline counterpart, Dan Sharpe had the potential to spring.

The other two men said little but fixed their gaze on Laurel until she wished they'd fall asleep or off the wagon or something. Yet she found nothing sinister in their stares, just a frank-eyed admiration. When she smiled they turned rosy and hastily averted their gaze.

A warm welcome, hot water for washing, and a clean bed after a bounteous supper that left her ashamed of her unusual appetite did much to restore Laurel's optimism. Besides, if Mrs. Greer could placidly knit in spite of the narrow ledges and rushing streams they crossed, the danger couldn't be as great as Laurel feared.

An eternity later, but actually a few days, the wagon swung around the same bend that had hidden Antelope from Adam's view months earlier. Little had changed except more people now thronged the dusty street and a few new cabins had been built. To Laurel's fascinated, horrified gaze any expectations or romantic beliefs about the hamlet died an instant death. Antelope itself showed what a mirage her ideas had been. Here lay naked substance, a small but sprawling town at her very feet.

Mrs. Greer, sensing Laurel's dismay, calmed the troubled girl's whirling brain. "Look up, child."

Laurel automatically obeyed. Jagged mountains guarded the town and offered security, something to cling to in this strange place. They felt like old friends, friendly in spite of their scarred, snow-clad surfaces. *Small wonder the Psalmist had looked to the hills for the strength that cometh from God,* Laurel thought.

She inhaled and felt a rush of exhilaration renew her inner self. No matter what lay ahead, or behind, no matter where she went or if she stayed, those mountains had been etched permanently into her heart, mind, and soul.

"You'll want to see the young doctor right

away," Mrs. Greer whispered when Dan Sharpe reined in his team.

Sheer panic destroyed her serenity. "Not yet," she said breathlessly. "I — I want to bathe and — and —"

"Of course." Mrs. Greer chuckled then frowned. "Hmmm. The hotel, such as it is, won't do for you. Let's see." Her face brightened and her double chins quivered. "The Widow Terry has a spare room since her daughter married. She's particular about who she takes in but she'll be glad for company."

Laurel had little chance to protest. Mrs. Greer swept her along in the falling dusk. They rounded a corner.

"Well, look who we're running into." Pleasure dripped from every word.

Laurel stared at the roughclad but unmistakable figure just ahead. Her intentions to dress up before letting Adam see her became futile. She gathered her travel-stained skirts in one hand, raced down the narrow lane off the main street, and clasped the dark-haired man's arm. Her heart pounded more from anticipation than exertion. "Hello!"

The man turned and looked into her face. "Excuse me, miss. You must have mistaken me for someone else."

Laurel nearly collapsed. Adam's steady

voice was denying her. She turned to stone.

"What's all this?" Mrs. Greer hurried up, her pleasant face distorted by shadows dancing in the dusk.

"This young lady seems to feel she knows me. I've never seen her before in my life." Swiftly and surely he removed Laurel's clutching, desperate fingers.

EIGHT

This couldn't be happening. Laurel had expected shock, disapproval, and even a reprimand from Adam but not a refusal to acknowledge their acquaintance and friendship! Her knees felt lifeless. Would they give way any minute?

"Now, Reverend Birchfield, how could you know her? This is Miss Brown, come all the way from West Virginia. She knows the doctor, and —"

The man Laurel belatedly realized was not Adam but an older version of him threw back his head and laughed. "And in this half-dark she thought she'd found him!" He laughed again and even in the dimness she could see Adam as he would be a few years from now. Relief and surprise left her stunned. At least Adam hadn't rejected her presence.

"I'm taking her to the Widow Terry's," Mrs. Greer said as she firmly grasped

Laurel's arm. "Tell Dr. Birchfield Miss Brown will see him in an hour or whenever he's free."

"Gladly, and a delayed welcome, Miss Brown." The minister whose voice and appearance so reminded Laurel of Adam left the two bewildered women.

"It will take a good hour for you to get freshened," Mrs. Greer said in her practical way. "Soon as I introduce you to Mrs. Terry I'll trot back and have Dan drop off your trunk. No girl wants to have her beau see her looking bedraggled from a long journey."

Again, Laurel didn't have the wits or bean to deny that Dr. Birchfield was her beau. All she wanted was time to settle down before he came.

Mrs. Terry turned out to be as welcoming as Mrs. Greer had foretold. She not only heated water and helped Mrs. Greer unpack Laurel's trunk — with many an *ooh* and *aah* — she quickly heated irons and pressed the fluffy pink gown. She also announced that she'd just walk a piece with Mrs. Greer since the doctor would be there to keep her new boarder company. "If you want to work, my dear, I can tell by your gowns you are a good needlewoman and I need help in my business."

"I'd like that." Laurel thought of her dwindling resources, the birthday and Christmas money now depleted by her journey.

The two chattering women, one billowy, one thin almost to the point of gauntness, but both unmeasurably kind, vanished through the door.

Ten minutes later a rapid knock on the peeled pine log door announced Dr. Birchfield's arrival and set Laurel shivering.

Every day Dr. Adam Birchfield lived and worked in Antelope he more clearly saw the need for his skills and rejoiced. How much more opportunity to give real service here than back home in Concord, especially since it had grown and attracted other doctors. The long rides out to ranches and the ever-changing Wyoming mountains, hills, and valleys continued to thrill him to the soul. He rode in at dusk one snowy afternoon, content and at peace.

A blast of music from the Pronghorn saloon, defiantly mocked by another from the Silver, upset him as usual, but much of his business stemmed from saloon patronage. He rode down the street, turned his mount, and trotted toward home, feeling more peaceful with each mile. Being here with Nat had turned out to be everything he had hoped for and more. Adam led his horse into shelter, quickly rubbed him down, and strode into the sweet-smelling log cabin.

"Hmmm," he sniffed, "something smells good."

Nat's wide white smile flashed. His dark eyes twinkled. "Venison stew, hot biscuits and —" He triumphantly waved a glass jar. "Wild berry preserves."

"Donated by a grateful parishioner?" Adam shrugged out of his snowy coat and boots before making for the welcome warmth of the fireplace with its roaring flames.

"Not exactly." Nat turned the tables on his brother and his sparkling dark eyes showed how much he enjoyed doing so. "Sally Mae Justice made them with her own little hands and wants our good doctor to have them. It's the only way poor little her can show her appreciation and respect for the man who saved her brother Mark." Instant contrition replaced Nat's faithful imitation of Sally Mae's simpering. "I shouldn't mock her. Sally Mae really loves that cowboy brother and I'm sure she'd be grateful to whatever doctor saved his life. Even if he weren't 'the best catch Antelope's seen in many a year,' " he couldn't help adding.

"Forget that stuff!" Adam growled, but a reluctant grin found its way over his storm-wet face the same way the kitten Inkblot, yet another gift, always found herself close to the hearth. "Besides, I'm only the *second* best catch, you know." He clasped his hands in a ridiculous pose, gazed skyward, and said in a high falsetto, "Isn't it just too, too wonderful that with all Mr. Birchfield has to do he's getting up a choir for Christmas?"

Nat's face turned red and he muttered something that clearly told Adam his brother knew what it was to have to minister to silly young women who trailed and set traps for him.

"With all the cowboys and ranchers around, why do the few nice young women concentrate on us?" Adam asked later. Filled with good food and the prospect of a free evening together — a rare occurrence — the brothers lounged in front of the fire, safe from the pelting storm.

"We represent the East many of them knew and they haven't yet started to realize some of the cowboys and ranchers out here are among the finest men on earth." Nat's eyes glowed and he leaned forward. "I don't mean the hard-riding, hard-shooting, loudmouthed showoffs. I mean those who will find a place in the pages of western history books. Not for deeds of daring but for their relentless refusal to let a new and untamed country beat them."

Adam's eyes opened wide at Nat's fervor. He shifted into a more comfortable position and stretched. A mighty yawn followed and he stumbled to his feet. "Guess our discussion will have to wait." He yawned again, so wide he wondered if he'd dislocate his jaw. "Nothing like a blizzard, hot food, and a warm fire to make a man sleep."

"Goodnight, Adam. I'm glad you came."

Adam gripped Nat's hand, strong as his own, yet never failing in kindness and blessing. "So am I."

An hour later he wondered at himself. *Why should he lie awake, reliving that poignant moment?* Wind shrieked around the corners of the cabin and through the treetops. The thud of snow too heavy for branches to bear sounded like intermittent small explosions. God grant he would not be needed this night. No man or horse could get in or out of town until the storm abated. Gradually the warmth of wool blankets and the well-banked fire did its work and Dr. Birchfield slept.

He awakened refreshed and to winter

beauty beyond words. Massachusetts had storms and snow, but Wyoming had outdone any Adam remembered. The first thing he noticed was stillness. Antelope had not yet dug itself out of the worst storm of the winter. His teeth chattering, Adam dressed in the warmest clothing Nat had provided, poked a single coal into fire, and eagerly clutched the mug of hot coffee his brother thrust into his hands. "Whew! This is welcome." Adam, who seldom drank the bitter brew, was overcome by the rich fragrance and warm comfort and drank heartily. "How cold is it?"

"Ten below. A real winter heat wave." Nat laughed out loud at Adam's astonishment. "It cleared off after the storm. Look." He pointed out the cabin window, whose bottom half lay packed with snow.

For one crushing, unexpected moment homesickness attacked Adam like a living, breathing thing. How many times had he eagerly peered from the window at Concord into such a snowy scene? Sleighing parties with jingling bells and laughing young men and women, clam chowder suppers and pumpkin pie with whipped cream no fluffier than the snowdrifts made Adam's insides twist.

A heavy but compassionate hand fell to

his shoulder. "I feel the same way. There hasn't been a winter since I left home that I haven't remembered Mother and Father, and you." The grip tightened and Adam had to strain to hear the next words.

"I wonder if I'll ever see them again."

A snowball-sized lump formed in Adam's throat and he blinked hard at the husky voice of his exiled brother. "We just have to keep praying that Father will realize. . . ." He couldn't continue and secretly welcomed the interruption when it came.

"Hey, Doc, Preacher! You fellers all right?" The stentorian yell effectively shattered the fragile moment.

Nat's hand fell and he strode to the door, pulled it open, and stepped back when a shower of accumulated snow fell.

"Well, I'll be!" Adam stared at the solidly packed wall of snow outside the door.

"We'll have you cleared soon," the same voice boomed. "Snow stopped before daybreak. Folks've been diggin' out ever since. Some of us figgered as how we better get you clear in case anyone needs marryin' or buryin' soon." Ribald laughter followed the remark.

"I doubt anyone will want either but thanks, boys. We'll have hot coffee for you when you break through," Nat promised at the top of his lungs before closing the door.

Faster than Adam expected the door burst open and a dozen lusty giants surged in out of the cold. They looked like the snow and ice statues Concord citizens built each winter.

"Don't mind the dripping," Adam told them. "We'll mop up when you're gone." He pushed the rescuers closer to the fire. "Is everyone all right?"

"Why shouldn't they be?" One big man raised his frosted eyebrows. "With this much snow not even the Pronghorn or Silver's open. Unless someone fell out of bed or something, you'll get no customers today, Doc." He took a long swig of coffee.

The prophecy proved false. Just after noon a half-frozen cowboy leading a lamed horse staggered to Adam's door and collapsed after pounding on it. It took time to get his story but Adam finally learned that Mark Justice was in trouble again.

"We g-got c-caught," the messenger gasped, trembling in spite of the hot drink Nat had helped Adam get down him. Shivers made his teeth chatter until his words blurred. "I th-thought he w-was right b-behind m-me." Unashamed tears fell, "M-my horse w-went d-down and wh-when I g-got him u-up, I c-couldn't find M-mark."

"Drink some more of this," Adam ordered, and he helped steady the mug.

Finally the cowboy could continue. "I hollered and heard an answer but it sounded far away." He gulped and stared at Adam. "When I found Mark he had a broken leg. We got to the line shack, God knows how. Probably because Mark keeled over from pain and I tied him in the saddle. Anyway, I did what I could after buildin' a fire and we slept some. But this mornin' Mark was out of his head with fever." His eyes still held shock. "I was scared to leave him and scared not to." He leaped up and almost fell, too exhausted to do more than plead. "He needs you, Doc. If you don't go, Mark's gonna die."

"I'll go." Adam set his mouth in a straight line. "Which line shack?"

"Follow my trail. It's a good five miles. Out toward the Lazy H but in the trees, not down by the river."

"I'll go with you." Nat reached for boots and coat.

"What about him?" Adam pointed at the patient who had sunk back once he had delivered the critical message.

"Be right back." Nat shouldered past him out into the brilliant day. Fifteen minutes later he appeared with a red-cheeked, well-bundled woman who took charge and shooed the brothers off on their difficult journey. "Land sakes, nothing wrong with this lad but worry and being tired. Go on."

"I knew I could count on Mrs. Greer," Nat said once they had decided snowshoes would be better than horses although it would take longer. "Best thing that ever happened to Antelope was when Greer set up his store and his wife stood right behind him." His tone turned somber. "It's going to take everything we have to save Mark."

"I know. I've been praying ever since the boy came."

Nat's radiant smile echoed Adam's statement but he said nothing. A long, tough trek lay before them. Wasting breath on talking could only make the ordeal worse.

The time of testing had come. Every ounce of muscle and strength gained in facing hard climbs and adverse conditions pitted itself against the worst odds known to humankind. A dozen times the young cowboy's words came back to Adam, tossed from the rising wind and spitting snow that heralded another storm.

We got to the line shack, God knows how.

Each time the words brought comfort, warming Adam's cold body that even the heaviest clothes and most strenuous exertion couldn't keep from chilling. Once he stumbled and noticed how quickly Nat came to lift him up, just as he lifts those who fall and stumble in life itself, Adam's dazed brain thought. He ploughed on, now leading and peering into the early gloom that had settled with the new storm at the rapidly filling tracks made by Mark Justice's partner. At other times, Adam simply followed in the footsteps of his big brother, as he had done so many times before. The journey became a parallel of life and tangled in it were the faces of two lovely young women from West Virginia.

"Think of something other than storm and whiteness," Adam ordered himself. He concentrated on Red Cedars. Would the Browns like the unusual gifts he had managed to find and have shipped? Ivy Ann's pert face, wide-open eyes, and smile when she saw the deerskin moccasins tantalized him. Laurel would like hers too. She probably wouldn't exclaim in Ivy's manner but Adam felt sure of Laurel's pleasure. Would the precious painting of Antelope Mrs. Hardwick had done at his insistence tempt the family to leave everything comfortable and come West? Adam's laughter at the way Ivy Ann and Laurel would set Antelope upside down drifted off with the wind. What would poor, silly Sally Mae think of the twins?

"Adam, stop!" A strong hand grabbed him. Nat looked like a snowman. He put his mouth close to Adam's ear. "You've passed the end of the footprints."

Adam looked down. A pang went through him. Dreaming of two gently bred young women had caused a lapse of concentration. He silently followed Nat back, chiding himself for his inattention. The treachery of this changeable land allowed no time to dream.

"Here!" Nat abruptly turned left. The footprints and hoofprints showed more clearly under the gigantic evergreens that had helped protect the ground from such heavy drifts. A little later Adam shouted with joy.

Through the fury of snow that proclaimed its defeat against the two travelers, a rude structure loomed, the line shack.

A lighted lantern, and a stirred fire later, Adam threw off his snowy outer clothing in one fluid motion. He bent over Mark Justice who tossed and muttered and whose hair lay in damp strands over a hot forehead.

"We have a fight ahead," he warned Nat.

"I know." Nat had already filled a large kettle with packed snow to melt and heat.

"What are his chances?"

"Better than when he had the bullet in him but not much."

Adam kicked off his boots and pulled on the heavy dry socks they'd brought in their packs. Then he opened his medical bag and went to work.

For three days the storm raged outside the lonely line shack, a monster ready to devour anyone caught in it. For three days a war raged inside the shack, the fight for a man's life. Adam didn't close his eyes for the first thirty-six hours and only consented to snatch a little sleep with Nat's firm promise to rouse him should there be the slightest change. Twelve hours later he awakened to find Nat bending over him and smiling broadly. "The fever's broken. The snow packs you used worked, thank God!"

Every trace of weariness and sleep fled before the good news. Adam bounded from bed. Never had Nat looked more beautiful than standing there unshaven and wrinkled, red-eyed but rejoicing. Careful nursing would bring Mark Justice back to the range again.

Limited by what supplies they had been able to carry, Nat made broth and tenderly fed it to the cowboy who was too weak to do it himself. Adam continued his almost twenty-four hour care, whistling to himself when Mark's gaze followed him.

"I don't know who really saved me," were the first words that came when Adam finally permitted Mark to speak. "If my pard hadn't gone for help or if you hadn't come —" His fingers nervously twitched the edge of the rough woolen blanket that covered him. He licked dry lips. "I-I reckon it was God."

Adam glanced sideways at Nat. Did he want to burst out with what lay in Adam's own heart? Would he, could he resist taking advantage of everything that had happened to bring Mark to God?

Before either brother could answer, Mark went on. "This is the second time." The dawning of understanding showed in his eyes and brightened them against the dark circles of illness.

Adam held his breath. Saying too much or too little might destroy the opportunity.

Nat smiled a singularly sweet smile at the cowboy. "Mark, you're very wise."

Red color stole through the white face to the roots of Mark's hair. "God must care a whole lot about me to send help and save my life twice." He straightened as if jabbed with a spear. "Why, it's three times, isn't it?" His eyes lighted and a weak smile crossed his face. "That time I came to church, you said God sent Jesus to save us, didn't you?" His gaze bored into Nat. He laughed, a kind of wild but happy laugh. "I read in a book that some folks in the world believe if you save someone's life that person belongs to you. I guess that means I belong to you — no, to God — and that I'll have to be riding with Him from now on?"

Nat's steady gaze never wavered. "That is up to you, Mark. The same way it's up to you whom you choose to bunk with and make your pard."

Tired out by the extra effort, Mark drooped back but before he closed his eyes he mumbled, "Gotta tell my pard we're gonna have a new trailmate from now on."

Adam's eyes stung. *What would Father and Mother and the Browns think if they could see into this line shack?* Would they realize how all the heartache and struggle fell away when measured against the soul of one wild cowboy?

NINE

The conversion of Mark Justice rocked Antelope. Nothing had set tongues wagging and heads nodding as much as the dramatic change in the cowboy once shot by the sheriff in self-defense. When the second storm abated and an unnatural warm spell followed, Nat went for help. Mark bit his lip to hold back the pain when his comrades lifted him onto a steady horse. The curses they expected to split the air never came. Blood ran down Mark's chin from where he had driven his teeth into his lower lip but he said nothing and stuck on the horse.

At his request, the men took him to the Lazy H bunkhouse instead of into town. "What's a little old broken leg?" he demanded once Adam pronounced the break clean and healing well. "You poor fish will have to be out checking on how many cattle got caught in the storm. I get to lie in bed or hobble around a nice warm bunkhouse, shoot the breeze with Cooky, and take me a va—cation." He didn't add what he told Nat later. "I'll have a chance to read the Bible you gave me. Now that I'm riding with God, I want Sally Mae to know about Him. She always did listen to what I have to say and she'll be coming around soon. I better get ready." He clutched the Bible and jauntily waved goodbye to the Birchfields.

More of the story came from other Lazy H hands.

"Crazy kid," one rangewise cowboy told Adam. "Never preaches. Just lays there readin' that Bible." He squirmed a bit then looked square into the doctor's eyes. "He told us everything that happened there in the line shack. Blamed if I didn't go and get a cinder in my eye just then and have to rub it out." He cackled. "A lot of the other men sat there rubbin' their eyes too. Guess it kinda got to us." He took a deep breath. "Makes a feller sort of wonder. I mean, Mark's never been out and out bad but you don't find them much wilder. He's shore changed."

"How come you never see Mark Justice around here no more?" became a standard question in Antelope.

"Aw, he's got religion," someone always answered, but a dozen times Nat or Adam saw the look in some of the other cowhands' eyes, the look that "made a feller sort of wonder."

"You know, Mark can be one of the best witnesses for Christ around here simply because he's one of the cowboys," Nat said one evening. "Any time a man or woman or child whose life isn't so spotless accepts the Lord, that person can be a powerful influence."

"I wonder how Mark can keep from preaching," Adam mused.

"I told him just to live it and baffle his friends!" Nat confessed.

Winter passed with a spate of spontaneous get-togethers with various Antelope families, the church program, and snow, snow, and more snow. The infrequent letters from Ivy Ann, always with a brief message Adam suspected Laurel tucked in secretly, brightened days made long and weary by the fight against cold, sickness, and accidents. Adam gloried in knowing if he hadn't been where God wanted him to be many of those who came down with pneumonia would surely be dead. If at times he longed for a companion, a wife, he quickly drowned the wish in the joy of being with his brother.

Suddenly, spring came, not stealing into

Antelope like a thief in the night, but with a rush of warm days that released rivers from their captivity and sent them gleefully chuckling, free from winter hibernation under sheets of ice. Tiny flowers sprang up. New life abounded and Adam lifted up his head and gave thanks. Only one sore spot remained: It had been a long time since he heard anything from his friends, the Browns, or from Mother, who faithfully smuggled letters to him. How had they kept through the winter? What news Antelope had came slowly and only after a long time. If it weren't for Dan Sharpe, who had already made one round trip out for a top-heavy load of supplies, the world since the snowfall might as well not exist!

One early evening Adam felt more tired than ever. If only his patients would follow his advice. At times he despaired of ever convincing these people that when he ordered rest it didn't mean after all the usual work chores ended. Yet he couldn't blame them. Every family busy with spring work toiled from sunup to past sundown. How could they do anything else when duty called?

Adam sighed, wishing Nat would return from whatever errand had called him out. The cabin felt empty without patients, or

Nat. Too tired to eat the warm supper he found saved for him by his thoughtful brother, Adam restlessly paced the floor longing for he knew not what.

Suddenly the door flung open and Nat came in, his mouth stretched wide in an expression of glee. He tossed his hat into a corner.

"You look like the Cheshire cat in *Alice in Wonderland,*" Adam told him, unreasonably resenting Nat's obviously high spirits when his own were mysteriously low.

"I've just seen a vision."

"You've *what?*" Adam was jolted out of his doldrums.

"Not a religious vision," Nat quickly amended, "but a vision of fair young maidenhood."

"Sally Mae's in town again?" Adam taunted while a quiver of anticipation went through him. "Since when is she a vision?"

"My good man." Nat drew himself up as if offended, but his twinkling black eyes ruined the attempt. "I am not referring to Sally Mae Justice. I am referring to a young and lovely young woman who pursued me down the street, clutched my arm, and looked into my face then said, 'Hello.' Furthermore, a young lady I have never seen before."

"Are you making this up?" Adam demanded, while that same odd lurch of his heart pumped blood against all reason.

Nat's keen look replaced his teasing. "No, Mrs. Greer explained it all. In the dim light the young woman mistook me for you."

"What young woman?"

"You haven't heard from Ivy Ann Brown for a long while, have you?" Nat grinned tormentingly with the expression that contrasted so to his serious demeanor when ministering.

"Impossible!" It burst from the depths of Adam's heart. He must be mad to think of it. *Yet wouldn't a stunt like this be just like Miss Ivy Ann Brown?*

"I am to tell you that Miss Brown will see you at the Widow Terry's where she has taken up residence in one hour, or whenever you're free."

It was all Adam could do to keep from rushing to Mrs. Terry's cabin. He bathed, shaved, and dressed in fresh clothing from the skin out. He ignored the gleam in Nat's eye and his innocent comment.

"Wish I had a pretty girl from the East to visit." A few minutes before the appointed time, he presented himself at the front door of Ivy Ann's new abode, willing his usually steady heart to stop pounding.

The pink gown swirled around Laurel's unsteady feet as she slowly walked to the door. She hesitated, one soft hand on the latch. Then she took a deep breath, lifted her chin with all her heritage of southern pride, and opened the door.

A tall, deerskin-clad figure stood before her.

Laurel's quick survey took in the new man. Dr. Adam Birchfield in the western garb he had adopted for comfort and practicality outstripped the young man in fine broadcloth and immaculate linen she remembered.

"Hello, Adam." Why did she stand frozen before the familiar stranger? She anxiously scanned his face, lean from hard work and outdoor calls, and felt relieved to discover the beginnings of a smile. Yet what shadow lurked in the watching dark eyes? It couldn't be disappointment, could it? Her spirits that had been shored up by the warm bath and the pink gown fell. The next instant the look vanished and laugh crinkles half-closed his eyes.

"Well, Miss Ivy Ann, you've done it this time! I thought you were the young lady who refused to give up the comforts of home for the good of our expanding country." He threw back his head and laughed, just as his brother had done in the street earlier.

An icicle pierced Laurel to her very soul. So Ivy Ann *had* won again, in spite of everything. She opened her mouth to cry out the truth, but was stopped by Adam's hearty voice.

"Don't look so stricken." He took her hand and shook it. Genuine welcome lightened his face. "It's wonderful for you to be here no matter what the reason." He led her to a settee and sat down beside her. "When I didn't hear from you for a time I thought you had probably forgotten all about your Wild West doctor friend."

"I could never do that." Laurel's lips moved of their own accord. Her mind ran in a dozen directions.

"How's Laurel? And your father and mother?"

With a tremendous effort the distraught girl managed to mumble, "All my family is well, or at least they were when I left." Inside she wanted to shriek. Any hope that the doctor had escaped Ivy's charms without regret faded when Adam continued.

"Nat told me how you mistook him for me in the dusk." Another laugh escaped.

"Would you like to know what else he said about you?"

"Why, of course." She nervously pleated her frothy pink skirt, hating it with all her heart and wishing she'd worn calico. Yet, would it have changed anything? Although Adam had heard her feelings about the West, never in a million years would he believe the quiet twin capable of the escapade she had just completed.

"It's still hard for me to believe you're here." Admiration shone in Adam's face. "Say, but we'll have a good time. I have places to show you that will make you turn traitor to even your beautiful Red Cedars." He went on making plans while Laurel numbly prayed for Mrs. Terry to return before she betrayed her identity. She must think and decide what to do. Laurel had been prepared for disapproval, even shock. She hadn't even considered that Adam would take her for Ivy Ann.

By pasting a smile over lips that wanted to tremble, she oohed and ahed in all the right places and knew how a prisoner given a reprieve must feel when the Widow Terry swept in, greeted Dr. Birchfield, pointedly looked at the clock, and ushered Adam out.

"She's going to be here for a spell. Now you get home and get your rest. The good

Lord knows there are few enough uninterrupted nights for you."

At last Laurel escaped from her landlady, if she could be called that when she obviously intended for Laurel to replace the daughter who had married and gone. In a tiny, piney-smelling room Mrs. Terry hastily cleared of cloth bolts and trims, Laurel stared out the single window at stars that looked near enough to pick. *What should she do now? Seek Adam out at the first opportunity and confess?*

She tossed and turned, remembering how above all else Adam hated deceit. Her courage failed. At least until she made new friends Dr. Birchfield must remain a staunch ally to whom she could turn in this faraway land. "If I can do all the wonderful things he has planned we'll be together," she comforted herself. "Dear God, it isn't that I won't tell him. I will, but just not now. Besides, I never said I was Ivy Ann. He said I was. I just didn't correct him." She moved again and kept her gaze on the majestic stars. "I know you hate deceit even worse than Adam does, but I just can't —"

Misery took over and the longing to be safely back at Red Cedars. She had thought nothing could be worse than living forever in her twin's shadow. Now the shadow of her own making lay long and dark over any chance for happiness in this forbidding land. A wail in the distance didn't help. A wolf? Coyote? She shivered under the warm, beautifully made quilts Mrs. Terry had brought out from her "saving for comp'ny" closet. Did everyone who broke free from home, especially those who slipped away without the family knowing, feel this way?

Before she finally slept, Laurel had wrestled with her knotty problem and decided she had no choice. Until she got close enough to Adam Birchfield to feel that he cared enough to forgive her, she must be Ivy Ann — not in what she said but in what she did. Perhaps he would attribute the differences she knew she could not hide to her being in a new place. Or maybe he had forgotten some of Ivy's little ways.

She sighed. All the times she had played parts in young people's entertainments hadn't prepared her for the monstrous role she faced in playing her own sister! Perhaps she should have corrected Adam immediately. The one other option lay in going home.

"No!" She sat upright in bed. A surge of protest drowned out the sensibility of that move. "I'm here and I'm staying." She slid back down under the covers and a hard core

of stubbornness formed within her. *So what if Adam built on his gladness to see Ivy Ann and fell in love? It would really be with her, Laurel, wouldn't it?* She fell asleep hugging the thought to her heart. If that happened, surely he would forgive her. . . .

Laurel hadn't counted on a new complication entering her already topsy-turvy plans. Blond-haired, amber-eyed Dan Sharpe had ideas of his own. Before Mrs. Terry and Laurel had finished breakfast the next morning, Dan rapped on the door.

Mrs. Terry's cup hit table with a little crash. Her thin face turned toward the door. "My, my, isn't your beau impatient?" She marched to fling open the door and welcome Dr. Birchfield, then scowled in surprise.

"Morning, Mrs. Terry." Early sun turned Dan's hair to molten gold.

"Land sakes, Dan Sharpe, what're you doing coming around here at the crack of dawn when a body's getting ready for work?"

"Just paying my respects. Is Miss Brown here?"

"Bees to the honeypot," Laurel heard her hostess mutter before she grudgingly allowed Dan to enter.

"I just wondered if you'd care to go riding

a little later," Dan drawled. "Every unmarried man around's going to come calling." He sent a significant glance at her bare ring finger. "According to Mrs. Greer, Doc has a prior claim but I don't see any sign of it being staked out."

In the middle of Mrs. Terry's indignant gasp Laurel coolly replied, "I don't quite understand your meaning, Mr. Sharpe, but it doesn't really matter. I am to help Mrs. Terry and my work begins immediately. I'll have little time to go riding, at least until I get settled," she amended when she saw his reaction. "I do appreciate your calling, however. It's nice to have the local people welcome me to my new home." The next instant she wished she had bitten her tongue.

"You plan to stay permanently?" Dan's gaze sharpened and drilled into her.

Again she thought of that tiger, under control but still dangerous. Laurel smiled in the way she had seen Ivy Ann do a hundred times, a smile guaranteed to disarm her inquisitive suitors. "Who knows?" She shrugged her shoulders in a dainty gesture. "I suppose much will depend on how I like Antelope. Now, if you'll excuse us, I'm sure it's time for Mrs. Terry and her new apprentice to go to work." She held out her hand.

Danger signals in Dan's eyes warned her the battle had neither ended nor been won but he merely bowed over her hand. "Remember, I asked first," he said, then bowed toward Mrs. Terry and swung out, whistling the first few bars of "Dixie."

"Well, of all the — I knew Dan Sharpe was presumptuous but this really beats it all!" Mrs. Terry's astonished reaction sent Laurel into a fit of giggles.

" 'Remember, I asked first,' " she mimicked. "Who does he think he is? I get the feeling he's convinced that any girl would just be waiting for him to confer attention on her."

"That's Dan Sharpe." Mrs. Terry's thin lips closed tightly. Then she added, "I'm not one to spread gossip but according to whispers there's a whole lot about Dan Sharpe no one knows. Or at least if they do, they aren't telling."

Laurel stopped, her hands filled with the breakfast dishes she had gathered up. She impulsively said, "Mrs. Terry, I'm a stranger in a strange land who's going to need a lot of help in understanding the people and the place. I really need you to guide me."

A pleased expression lighted the older

woman's face. "I think we're going to get along real well, child. Real well." She folded the breakfast cloth, shook it outside the cabin door, and smiled in a way that did more to settle Laurel down than anything since she left West Virginia.

TEN

"I like your Ivy Ann," Nat told Adam one late spring afternoon. The brothers had reined in on top of a grassy knoll above Antelope to let their horses rest after a climb. "I wouldn't have thought such a girl as you described could so quickly adjust and become part of the community." His fine eyes looked into the blue heavens. "But something seems to be troubling her. Have you noticed the way she bubbles at times and still carries an almost brooding look at others?"

Adam relaxed in his saddle. "Yes, it's strange. The Ivy Ann I knew at Red Cedars cared for little except getting her own way." His lips curved in remembrance. Aspen leaves decked in new-leaf green whispered secrets not to be shared with the riders. A confession Adam wanted to make halted on his lips and a worry line formed between his dark brows. Even though the Bible said to share burdens, right now Nat didn't need a heavier load. Nat's efforts to get more law and order than Antelope wanted had resulted in bitterness, especially from the owners of the Pronghorn and Silver saloons.

Suddenly Adam's horse shied and Nat's whinnied. Like a stab of lightning, a dark form appeared in front of the startled brothers. Adam's mouth fell open. A magnificent Indian warrior, powerful and naked to the waist, calmly grabbed the reins of both horses.

"Who — what — ?" Adam sputtered as fear gnawed at him.

"What do you want?" Nat took charge.

"Grey Eagle." The Indian pointed to himself. "You come." He pointed to Adam, then Nat. "Son sick, maybe die. Running Deer no die! You medicine man. Make well."

In bits and pieces they learned Grey Eagle's story. When the tribes had been rounded up and forced to go on reservations, a small band refused and hid in the vast wildness of the Wind River area. The government could spare neither the time nor troops to find and capture the wily group. They moved from time to time and lived as their ancestors had lived for hundreds of years, free and drifting.

Grey Eagle, who seemed to know more

about the area's happenings than the Birch-fields, had discovered the presence of a white medicine man in Antelope. He had tucked the information away, perhaps never intending to use it. In desperation, he refused to accept the death sentence his tribe's medicine man prescribed and now stood before Adam on behalf of his son.

"You go with me. Both go."

Adam didn't hesitate a moment. "Of course we'll go with you, Grey Eagle. When I became a doctor I promised to go any-where and to anyone who needed me." He held out his hand to show his good faith.

The dull black eyes glowed with dark fire and Grey Eagle took Adam's hand. "No tell where you go?"

Adam looked at Nat who quietly ex-plained, "Grey Eagle is putting the safety of his tribe in our hands." With slow move-ments he loosened the catch of his saddle-bag and took out his worn black Bible. "Grey Eagle, do you know what this is?"

"Great Spirit book."

Nat nodded. "My brother and I pledge by the Great Spirit we call God not to tell." He placed his and Adam's hands on the Bible.

Grey Eagle grunted and the semblance of a smile creased his aged, angular face. Without a word he slid into a cluster of trees and reappeared riding a shaggy horse, his only saddle a worn blanket. "Come."

Hours later they reached their destination, a cragbound valley only the tribe who called it home or an eagle on the wing could find. Ice-cold water bubbled from a spring, so cold Adam's teeth ached when he flung himself to the banks and drank. Spring flowers sent thrusts of color through the rich, green grass. A dozen tepees made up the village and horses grazed nearby. Grey Eagle led the brothers to the largest tepee. Wailing sounds sent chills through Adam. *Had they come too late?* He followed Grey Eagle and Nat into the smoky interior. A stripling Indian lay on a bed of rich skins. Sweat glistened on his copper skin. The look in his eyes when he turned toward his father pierced Adam's heart. Terror, pain, and hope combined in the age-old expression that binds father and son.

"White medicine man." A sinewy arm drew Adam nearer.

A cry of rage from the howling Indian medicine man was cut short with a single wave of Grey Eagle's mighty arm.

"Clear everyone out," Adam ordered Nat with such authority in his voice the huddle of Indians silently obeyed without question.

Adam quickly examined Running Deer.

"You'll have to help, Nat." His lips felt stiff. "We've got a red-hot appendix."

"Not again!"

Adam nodded. "Just like Mrs. Hardwick." He pressed the lower right area of Running Deer's abdomen. A moan of pain escaped the tightly clenched teeth.

"You make well." Grey Eagle stood to one side, his arms folded across his chest. A muscle in his drawn face showed his love for his only son, now lying defenseless against the white medicine man's probing.

Adam straightened and fearlessly looked into the dark wells of Grey Eagle's eyes that had seen bloodshed and peace, sunrise and sunset. "I will do all I can and my brother will ask the Great Spirit to help me."

"Bad spirit in son."

"We must let it out." Adam compressed his lips. What a setting for his second emergency appendectomy since reaching the Wyoming Territory! He quickly made what preparations he could, calling for boiling water and the tepee flap left open for extra light. Then with the most fervent prayer he had ever offered, he began.

Grey Eagle unflinchingly watched the thin red line that followed Adam's initial incision. He gave not a sign of inner turmoil yet both Adam and Nat knew how torn he must be. To go against his medicine man's advice, to let a white man cut his son, had been a terrible decision.

Again the years of training and prayers met to triumph. Again, the diseased appendix burst, but outside of the patient. Humility and thankfulness filled Adam and he quickly sutured and bandaged. "Nat, I want you to go back and leave me here for a few days. I have to be sure Running Deer gets the proper care." Adam stretched to full height. "Grey Eagle, I believe your son will live but I want to stay with him."

Grey Eagle solemnly nodded and turned toward the open tepee flap. "Tell tribe." A string of unfamiliar phrases followed his exit from the makeshift operating room.

"Why don't I stay too?" Nat frowned.

"And miss your Sunday services? Antelope would have a search party out!" exclaimed Adam as he washed his stained hands in the clean water Nat brought. "Give me a week, will you? If anything's going to develop, it will by then." He watched Nat ride off with Grey Eagle, who would make sure he could find his way back, then called a warning. "Don't tell everything. Just say I'm staying with an out of town patient, will you?"

Nat signaled and disappeared after Grey Eagle.

Of all the experiences so far, the week in the small and hidden Indian camp affected Adam most deeply. Running Deer's young body healed incredibly fast. Adam spoke through him and his father to the old medicine man and pleased the ancient by carefully listening to what he had to say. Certain herbs and primitive knowledge made good medical sense and he gratefully expressed his appreciation. By the time Nat returned, Adam felt a certain reluctance to leave, although eager to get back to their own place. When they did go, they carried the pledge of the tribe's eternal friendship and gratitude.

Adam had also found time to think while in the hidden village. The problem he'd concealed from Nat came out into the open of Adam's mind and had to be dealt with. Ivy Ann's face danced in the firelit shadows, but so did another. After prayer and much consideration, Adam set his jaw firmly. The showdown with Ivy Ann had to come soon, for both of their sakes.

Laurel had, as Nat said, settled into Antelope the way a broody hen settles into her nest. Her moments of homesickness had little chance against the enticement of spring in the Wyoming Territory. Although

155

sensible enough to know part of the masculine attention could be credited to lack of competition, she couldn't help rejoicing over the unqualified approval of most single Antelope males. She treated them all alike, to Dan Sharpe's chagrin and Mrs. Terry's secret delight, and she never acted like Ivy Ann to anyone except Adam — and only when she remembered.

Sally Mae and the few other girls loved Laurel in spite of their jealousy. As Sally Mae told her brother Mark, who was one of Laurel's most faithful admirers, "It'd be different if she was flirty or stuckup. She's just nice to everyone."

The only real flaw in Laurel's world except for running away from her beloved Red Cedars was the weight of deceiving Adam. It pricked at her like an imbedded splinter. *Soon,* she often promised herself, but days and then weeks passed and she still had not confessed to Adam and asked his forgiveness.

During that time the respect and attraction that had lighted a tiny fire in her heart grew into the steady flame of love. Although Adam could not suspect it, he had no rivals for Laurel, alias Ivy Ann. She also saw in his eyes when she caught his gaze in unguarded moments a growing feeling and she thanked God for it.

Widow Terry's business took a surprising jump after Laurel signed on as her apprentice. "You're my best advertisement," Mrs. Terry told the young woman. She eyed the tiny frills around the high neck and long sleeves of Laurel's work gown.

Laurel laughed. "Back home we — I learned to make the best of what we had and make sure I took care of it! New gowns can't compete with the need for new tools, seed, and all the things that wear out on a big farm." She industriously leaned closer to the window to catch a final gleam of daylight. The soft glow of lamplight didn't offer adequate light for the tiny stitches necessary to finish Mrs. Hardwick's new Sunday dress, a dark blue gown with fine tucks and a wisp of braid on the collar.

"Ivy Ann?"

Something in Mrs. Terry's voice stilled the flying fingers. "Yes?" She felt guilty answering to the name she'd never claimed.

Dull red suffused the gaunt face. "I don't want to pry but hasn't Dan Sharpe been around an awful lot lately?" She rushed on, obviously eager not to offend. "Some of the other boys come too, but. . . ."

Laurel sighed, "I can't very well ask Dan not to drop by. I avoid him when I can and turn down twice as many of his invitations as I accept." She impatiently shook her head until a light brown curl escaped its mooring and hung over her forehead, making her look like a troubled little girl.

"I know, child." Mrs. Terry took up the child's dress she had cut out earlier then folded it and put it away. "Tomorrow's time enough for this." Her sigh matched Laurel's and her kind face seemed strange without her quick smile. "I guess as long as you aren't spoken for the boys won't leave you alone."

Laurel felt warmth steal into her cheeks. She bent her head, wishing she could confide in her new friend but rejecting the idea immediately. Not until she settled things with Adam could she tell anyone else. She pretended far more interest in setting the final stitches in the gown than she felt. "There! Dear Mrs. Hardwick will get a lot of service out of this dress and I know she'll look nice in it."

The keen-eyed dressmaker took the garment from Laurel and examined every seam and the set of the sleeves. "If I'd known what a good apprentice I'd get, why, I reckon I'd have sent back to West Virginia for you long ago!" She smiled roguishly. "But I s'pose a handsome young doctor is a better reason to come West than an old lady like me."

"You aren't old and I love you." Laurel hugged Mrs. Terry. Her words and action so flustered the widow the subject changed, as Laurel intended it would.

Only to Laurel did Nat confide his and Adam's adventure with Chief Grey Eagle and his people. She had learned to appreciate Antelope's minister and gloried in the fact that as Adam grew older, the same sterling qualities would deepen in his own life. Her first letter home actually spoke more about Nat than Adam. She praised his dedication to duty and devotion to his Lord and merely said Adam stayed extremely busy supporting his brother's spiritual ministry with physical healing. So when Nat called one evening while Adam was still in the hidden village, she gladly walked with him and thrilled to his tale.

"What's it like, the Indian village, I mean?" Laurel's sincerity loosened Nat's tongue.

"It's located in probably the most beautiful spot in Wyoming, inaccessible except to those who know the way. Even after going and coming back, guided by Grey Eagle, I'll have to look sharp when I go back for Adam. He could have simply had Grey

Eagle guide him but he wants me to pack in a few luxuries for the tribe — candy, bright cloth, that kind of thing."

She stopped short, her heart pounding at her own daring. "Take me with you when you go. I'd love to see the camp and meet Grey Eagle and Running Deer and their people." She clasped his arm with both hands.

For a moment she thought he'd agree but then he shook his head. Regret clouded his eyes. "I can't, Ivy Ann. I'm sorry."

"Why?" she persisted. "Don't you think I can ride or hike that far?"

He threw his head back and laughed in the way the Birchfield men did when highly amused. "Gracious, it isn't that. Antelope's rampant with stories of your horsemanship." His eyes twinkled with mischief. "Did you really beat Dan Sharpe in a race a few days ago?"

"Who told you?" She clapped her hand to her mouth then joined in his laughter. Pride lent a tilt to her chin, a sparkle to her mobile, face. "He was so sure he could beat me he offered me a headstart. I told him I needed no favors." She blushed, remembering how Dan suggested a wager, silver dollar against a kiss. She had coldly told him she didn't wager, then beat him in the race by a full three feet.

Now she returned to her teasing. "Please take me."

Nat shook his head again, more decidedly this time.

"Adam and I gave our word we would not reveal where the camp lies. I couldn't break that promise, although I'm sure you would enjoy the hard climb and scenery." A new thought brightened his face. "Tell you what. When I see Grey Eagle again I'll ask him for permission to have you visit the camp sometime. There's no guarantee he will agree but I can ask."

"Tell him he has nothing to fear from me," she said earnestly.

"I don't know about that." Nat's laughing mouth reminded her of Adam's. "According to Mark Justice and some of the other boys you are mighty dangerous. Seems a rash of heart trouble has broken out since you came."

His meaning brought floods of color to Laurel's neck and face. She controlled the desire to retort and meekly suggested, "Perhaps they should consult Dr. Birchfield."

"Perhaps they should," he blandly agreed, and Laurel wondered if the innocent words held a subtle, hidden warning.

On a soft spring evening a week after Adam came back to Antelope he called on Laurel. For the first time he seemed restless and uneasy. After a short while Mrs. Terry took up her bonnet and decided to "visit Mrs. Greer for a spell."

Disturbed by the change in Adam, Laurel couldn't help dreading the inevitable conversation that must follow. Somehow he must have discovered her deception. Perhaps Ivy Ann had written, not knowing her twin's masquerade. Yet through the dread came relief. At least things would be clear between them.

"I have something I must tell you," Adam began. Embarrassment colored his tanned face. "It's hard to say without sounding pompous.

"Ivy Ann, I've really enjoyed spending time with you. You are so different from the girl I met in West Virginia. But I have to be honest with you, even though you may despise me for it. I hope we can continue to be *friends*." His voice underscored the word.

"You seemed so bound to your home that I never dreamed you'd come to the Wyoming Territory. Since you arrived I've to convince myself — Ivy Ann, when you used to write to me your sister always included a message. At first I had the two of you all mixed up together." He drew in a long breath and stood to full height.

"What I'm trying to say is that I do admire you, especially since you've become part of Antelope. But I've had time to think. I know now I fell in love with Laurel the first time I saw her. I don't know if she would ever consider me or leave West Virginia, but maybe someday." He looked at her bent head. "Forgive me if in any way I've hurt you, Ivy Ann."

He loves me. He wants to marry me.

Laurel wanted to shout it to the peaks and let them echo back to the valley. Exquisite delight she hadn't known existed burst into a beautiful flower.

But it died on its stalk, frozen by reality. Ivy Ann still stood between them. Not a flesh and blood Ivy Ann, but the shadowy twin whose name Laurel wore like a crown of thorns.

Eleven

From the moment Ivy Ann Brown discovered Laurel had fled everything about Red Cedars changed. Sometimes she wondered how she could have been so blind. "Shallow, foolish, vain!" she accused herself. "Why didn't I see it sooner, before my flirting and hatefulness drove Laurel away?"

Days and nights of soul-searching agony thinned Ivy to string bean proportions and left dark smudges beneath her deep brown eyes. Gradually the beaux who had once delighted her and fallen in droves for her charms deserted, lured away by jollier and more interesting girls. She cared little. Even when Beauregard Worthington's calls became fewer and fewer "due to the press of business" she only shrugged.

"Why didn't I know how much I loved Laurel and how good she was until she left?" Ivy wailed to her parents.

For perhaps the first time, they offered no

excuses, no solace. "Most of the time we let the real treasures we have slip away and don't realize their worth," Thomas Brown sternly told his repentant daughter. He softened at the acute misery in her face. "We can't undo the past but we can use it to shape the future."

Sadie also suffered. Shocked by the defiance and secretiveness of her tractable Laurel, she haunted the front porch whenever anyone rode in from Shawnee. Laurel's first letter brought a certain uneasy peace.

"Thank God she's all right!" Thomas swept Sadie into a rare public embrace.

"She's happy, too," Sadie decided out loud once the letter had been read and reread. "This Mrs. Greer and Mrs. Terry sound like wonderful Christian women. Besides, Dr. Birchfield will look after her."

Thomas drew shaggy eyebrows together. "It doesn't excuse her going as she did."

"Would you have allowed her to go if she had asked?" Ivy Ann posed, not in her usual pert manner but seriously.

"Of course not!" Thomas faced west and a slow smile lightened his craggy features. "I didn't think she had it in her."

Every letter brought glowing reports of the beauties of the Wyoming Territory. Each message invited, not in words, but with the challenges Laurel had found. Coupled with her experiences, the memory of Adam Birchfield's strong views on the need for godly men and women to help settle the West merged and clung.

Ivy Ann could see the effect of the long family discussions, first on her father, then on her mother, and last of all on herself. Inspired by her complete confession to God asking for His forgiveness, she found herself tantalized and drawn by the vastness of the unknown frontier that had swallowed Laurel. She also missed her twin with every fiber of her being. *Strange, she had always believed Laurel relied on her.*

Not one of the three Browns could remember when the tone of the conversation changed from, "If we should ever" to "When we get to Wyoming. . . ."

"Shall we write and tell Laurel?" became the hotly debated question. Thomas favored a blunt admission that through business connections he'd arranged to buy a ranch near Antelope and that Red Cedars had been eagerly snatched up by some of Beauregard Worthington's contacts.

Ivy Ann definitely wanted to surprise her twin. She had begun and discarded a dozen letters to tell Laurel how much she had changed. None came close to what lay in her heart. "I need to look into her eyes so she will know it is true," she told her parents.

Sadie remained undecided about telling Laurel but sang louder than ever while she did the hundreds of things necessary to turn over the property to its new owners. Many a tear dampened her work apron at the thought of leaving Black-eyed Susan, Gentian, and their families. Yet her sturdy pioneer spirit rose up and sustained her. Soon she would be a part of the new flood of expansion sweeping America, and soon she would see Laurel.

At last Ivy Ann persuaded her mother to side with her and Thomas reluctantly gave in. Laurel would not be told.

"Just think of her face when we knock on Mrs. Terry's door and ask for Miss Brown." Ivy Ann gleefully clapped her hands. Sincere and repentant she might be, but her unquenchable spirit of fun had bounced back like an India rubber ball.

A flurry of farewell parties with a dozen suitors wondering how they could temporarily have thought Ivy Ann dull swept by until the perfect June morning when the Browns turned their backs on Red Cedars and faced west.

The long train journey offered time to

hear all the details of the new life that lay ahead. Thomas looked ten years younger, so fired was he with enthusiasm and vigor. "The ranch we're getting is actually part of one of the largest spreads near Antelope."

Ivy hid a smile at the word *spread.* Ever since they started talking of going West, western colloquialisms, courtesy of Mr. Hardwick, sprinkled her father's conversation.

"Mr. Hardwick, who owns the Lazy H, had such terrible losses due to the unusually cold winter he's been forced to sell or go under," said Thomas as he took writing materials from his bag and drew squiggly letters. "This is the Lazy H cattle and horse brand. See? The *H* is lying down on the job."

"What will our brand be?" Ivy Ann peered at the paper with interest.

"Hardwick suggested we use the Double B." Thomas drew another figure, ℬℬ. "It will be easy to brand over the Lazy H because it only needs a few curves to change."

Sadie looked worried. "I'm not sure I like a purchase where we don't know the seller. What if he cheats us or doesn't furnish as many cattle as the contract calls for? We put most of what we got from Red Cedars into this."

"My dear, this Hardwick is so well thought of and trusted on the range that every person our agent talked with flared up at the idea he'd ever cheat anyone. Most of them just do business with a handshake and Hardwick's never been known to go back on his word." When Sadie didn't look totally convinced, Thomas continued. "Besides, it isn't like we're going into partnership. The sections of range we just bought are separated from the Lazy H by a small parcel of land owned by someone else. That's one reason Hardwick let some of his holdings go." A frown flickered. "I kind of wish we were snuggled up to the Lazy H but, according to my man, whoever owns the in-between strip of land has never done anything with it except collect fees for grazing of Lazy H cattle."

Any time interest in the changing scenery lagged, the fascinating subject of the new Double B rose to be explored.

State after state surrendered to the steady *clack-clack* of the train's churning wheels until as Adam and then Laurel had done the Browns gazed in awe at the Rocky Mountains and knew their destination could not be far off. Like the two travelers before them, the clear distance deceived Thomas, Sadie, and Ivy Ann.

Once Ivy cried out, "Look! Those must be the pronghorns Adam told us about." Spellbound, the easterners watched a small band standing with raised heads and staring intently at the train. A heartbeat later, they moved into single file and fled faster than anything the Browns had ever seen.

"They can reach speeds of up to sixty miles an hour," a fellow passenger told the enthralled travelers.

Ivy Ann pressed her nose to the train window until the last of the graceful animals disappeared from sight. *Would the rest of the Wyoming Territory prove as new and intriguing?* The answer would come soon enough.

Adam's declaration of love for a girl he believed safely back home in West Virginia changed Laurel's troubles to disaster. All the sweetness of being loved by the finest man she had ever known turned sour because of her deception. The sword of Damocles that legend said once hung by a single hair paled next to the weight pressing down on Laurel.

Tell him, her conscience ordered night and day.

I can't, her weaker side protested. *What if he despises me and I lose his love?* Yet even the weak side had no answer to conscience's retort.

How is waiting going to help? You have to confess sometime.

So she stitched seams and hemmed gowns, smocked and tucked, and tried to ease her conscience and aching heart that leaped each time she saw Adam. How hard was the way of a deceiver! Basically honest, Laurel hated the role she played yet feared what Adam would say. His integrity that first won her respect then love worked against her now.

Just a few more days, she promised herself, then the days stretched into weeks. Early summer came in all its Wyoming glory and Laurel still had not confessed.

While she struggled, so did Adam to his own amazement. He had been so sure of himself about Laurel and his feelings he confidently expected every worry would slide away regarding the future. Nothing prepared him for the tumult that continued to rage inside him, stilled only by Antelope's demands on him for skill and comfort.

"I never dreamed Ivy Ann could change so," he told his horse a dozen times. "All the wonderful qualities I saw in Laurel are magnified in Ivy since she came!" As he raised his face toward the blue heavens where fleecy clouds played tag, he prayed, "Dear God, can a man be in love with two women at the same time?"

His question remained unanswered and a startling happening drove it and other things from Adam's mind. News came that the Rock Springs bank had been robbed. Antelope perked up its ears, especially when the amazing truth came out: No masked men had appeared. No dynamite or the usual paraphernalia of such robberies had been used. Someone, evidently in broad daylight, had simply marched in without being observed and helped himself. Or some wily, unauthorized person had a key and had come at night.

Rumors flew like cawing crows. Good citizens shook their heads and wondered. If anyone had information, it stayed locked behind securely fastened lips.

Following the robbery ranchers reported missing cattle and horses. Not in large numbers but enough that at first the range riders simply felt they'd drifted into draws. Horses known for their speed and endurance mysteriously escaped from corrals.

Hardwick reached the point of near explosion. "Here I've sold a piece of land and a stated number of animals in good faith," he said as he scratched his grizzled head. "Doc, it beats me how these dirty skunks can sneak in, cut out the best, and get away without someone seein' them." He held his muscular arm steady while Adam cleansed a nasty cut and dressed it.

"You say you've sold part of the Lazy H?"

"Had to." The terse reply said everything. "A few more hard winters like this one and I'd be out of ranching." He fumbled with the button on his sleeve.

"Who bought it?"

"Some feller from back —"

"Hey, Doc!" The door opened and a freckle-faced, gap-toothed boy burst in. "You're needed at the Pronghorn. Right now. There's been a fight an' a bunch of guys are about dead!" He slammed back out.

Adam grabbed for his medical bag and overtook the excited youngster halfway to the saloon. Sometimes he felt like refusing to patch up men who fought for entertainment or because they wouldn't take anything off anyone else. He shook his head and lengthened his stride. Never in his life had he turned his back on need and he couldn't start now, no matter how disgusted he might be.

When he stepped inside the saloon, a strangely silent crowd parted like the Red

Sea and fell back to make a path for him.

"Who's hurt worst?" He rolled up his sleeves and started to work, relieved that no one was "about dead" after all. When he had set a broken arm, stanched the blood from a head wound, and tended to various cuts and bruises he faced the motley group. "How many more of you are going to wind up like these men? Or like those?" He pointed out the open window toward the little cemetery at the end of town. "Don't any of you have brains enough to know that brawling settles absolutely nothing?"

"Sounds like we've got two preachers in this town instead of just one," a lazy voice drawled.

Adam whipped around, furious at the contemptuous comment. Dan Sharpe lounged in a chair tipped back against the wall with the two front legs in the air. Voices nervously tittered but the laughter Adam might have expected never came.

"I'm no preacher but I'm fed up with this kind of thing." His deadly quiet voice stilled the shuffle of feet that had greeted his outburst.

The chair came down in a hurry. Dan bounded up like a tiger, and his mirthless grin made the resemblance even more striking. Every curve of his tensed body showed all he needed to spring was a single word from Adam. "Trying to make Antelope a better place for — the ladies?"

His meaning was absolutely clear. Everyone in Antelope knew Dan Sharpe had fallen for Ivy Ann Brown like a second-rate rider. Even those who admired Dan muttered an inaudible protest that spurred Adam into action. Black rage erased his hatred of violence. In two quick steps he reached Dan, snatched a handful of deerskin shirt, and threw the shorter man back in his chair.

Faster than hail Dan reached for the gun hanging low on his right hip. Before it cleared the holster a mighty kick crumpled him into stomach-clutching misery and disabled him. In silence Adam Birchfield turned his back and strode out of the Pronghorn. A moment later he came back in. "He may have a broken rib or two. If he does, haul him down to my office."

For a time Antelope held its breath and waited. How would Dan respond? No one knew, not even his most trusted henchmen. His ribs had not been broken. Neither had he suffered permanent damage except to his ego. Three days later he stepped from the saloon just as Adam and Nat came out of the Greers' general store.

"Hold on there!" he called, and rapidly walked down the dusty street.

Adam and Nat froze. Unarmed, they could only watch Dan advance. Faces popped into windows. Men, women, and children on the street scurried for shelter from the inevitable fight. Nat involuntarily started to step forward and shield his brother but an iron hand restrained him as Adam's hoarse voice ordered, "No, this is my fight."

To the town's astonishment, Dan stopped a few feet from the brothers, took off his hat with his left hand, and held out his right. His clear voice reached everyone around. "Sorry, Birchfield. I was way out of line. No hard feelings?"

A little warning bell inside Adam told him not to trust Dan Sharpe any farther than he could see. Yet he had no choice but to accept the proffered hand. Someone coughed and a few cheered. Others looked disappointed at being cheated of a fight. But Dan clapped his hat back on his head, grinned a snowy grin, and marched into the Silver saloon.

Adam overheard one old-timer mutter, "That devil! Knows even the worst of us won't stand for some things. Now he walks off like a hero." A stream of dark brown tobacco juice pinged against a rock in the road. "Hope Doc's smart enough not to be fooled by that coyote in the chicken coop." He came over to Adam, walking with the uneven, bowlegged gait of a man more used to straddling a horse than hoofing it. "Sonny, don't you never turn your back on Dan Sharpe." He went on down the street before Adam could answer.

"I'm afraid you've made an enemy," Nat told him soberly.

Adam shrugged. "It won't be the last, I'm sure." He unseeingly gazed off down the street then looked up at the mountains. "Like you told me before I came, it's a rough land out here."

"You haven't changed your mind about staying?" Nat asked.

"No, but I've sure changed my mind about myself." Adam's clear laugh rang out. "I always felt I could be in control of any situation. Now I know that underneath the surface lies more anger than I ever dreamed possible!"

Before long the incident had slipped into the graveyard of stale news. Nat and Adam continued with their busy lives. Dan took advantage of the summer months to widen and better the rough wagon track into Antelope. Laurel gathered her courage to speak a dozen times and finally promised herself that the next time Adam came to see her she would trust in his love and tell him the truth. She secretly rejoiced when that time of reckoning was postponed due to a rash of illnesses and minor accidents.

One golden afternoon loud shouts brought her and Mrs. Terry to their cabin door. "Dan Sharpe's back," rang in the streets.

Widow Terry's face lightened. "Ivy Ann, go see if he brought back our bolts of cloth, will you?"

Glad to escape her own thoughts, Laurel lightly ran over to the main street. She saw Adam hastening toward the general store and she waved. He raised his hand, smiled, and froze when a familiar figure in a blue dress alit from Dan Sharpe's wagon.

She straightened her hat, and looked inquiringly around her. Suddenly she caught sight of the pink-clad statue whose hand remained upraised. "Laurel!" Ivy Ann gathered her skirts around her and sped down the street. "Surprise! We're here for good!"

Laurel watched her twin come as if in a dream. Surely it couldn't be happening, just when she had promised God to make things right with Adam, no matter what the cost.

Yet it *had* happened. She had waited too long.

Twelve

The arrival of the real Ivy Ann Brown and her parents — and the untangling of why Laurel had chosen to masquerade as her twin — offered an even more interesting topic of discussion than the Rock Springs bank robbery. After the first initial shock, when Adam's heart had cried out in gladness at the sight of that blue gown, he fell prey to more emotions than he had known existed: disillusionment that the young woman he had put on a pedestal could have deceived him; joy that the real Laurel was not Ivy Ann; and wariness in his dealings with either twin. When Nat began squiring Laurel, all he felt was jealousy, pure and simple.

Dan Sharpe soon transferred his affections. Ivy Ann's welcome of him as part of her new life soothed the blow to his vanity that Laurel had dealt with her indifference. He even accompanied Ivy to church at her insistence. Caught up in gladness over being with Laurel again, Ivy took to the range like a rabbit to its burrow. Never a Sunday afternoon passed but what the wide porch of the old ranchhouse on the Double B was crowded with riders in their best.

During the week Ivy Ann rode with whatever hand she could pry loose from her father's iron supervision. To the family's amazement, Laurel preferred to stay in town with Mrs. Terry and keep her job until winter when the married daughter and son-in-law planned to come back, build onto the cabin, and live with the kindly woman.

"I started a job and I'd like to finish it," she wistfully told her parents. She didn't add that even glimpses of Adam rewarded her diligent search for him every time she went out. Or that Nat offered strong support. He had come the same evening her family arrived and asked to see her alone.

"It's been a terrible shock but I believe that in time he will forgive you," Nat comforted. "In the meantime, may I accompany you now and then?" He added irrelevantly, "That sisters of yours could be quite a woman if she were more like you."

At last they arranged things so Laurel would go home weekends but stay in town during the week. Before long and in spite of her own preoccupation, Laurel saw small signs that convinced her Nat had fallen in love with Ivy Ann. Poor Nat! Although she could see some changes in Ivy, the chances she would ever consider marrying a minister were a thousand to one. Nat never expressed his feelings but Laurel felt sure she saw them in his dark, expressive eyes.

"Ivy Ann," Laurel said one Sunday evening just before she left to ride back to Antelope, "I don't want to interfere but you do know Dan Sharpe is in love with you?"

"As if any decent girl could care for him," Ivy scoffed and shook her light brown curls until they danced. "He is so stuck on himself I wouldn't be surprised if he tries to tell God when to make the sun come up and go down!" A shrewd look made her appear far older than almost twenty-one. "Besides, Sally Mae said Dan was crazy about you. The only reason he likes me is to get back at you for turning him down."

"Don't be foolish." Laurel blushed.

Ivy Ann stretched her round white arms, bare to the elbow. "You know who I think is the nicest man out here?"

Adam, Laurel's aching heart cried. She sat up straight on her sister's bed.

"Nathaniel Birchfield." Warm color added beauty to the lightly tanned face and her dark eyes shone. "I know he'd never look at me and I could never be good enough for him, but I do admire him. He's so much like Adam, and then some."

Laurel felt relief pour through her. Just having Ivy not interested in Adam meant a lot. She considered dropping a hint to her twin and changed her mind immediately. *Once before she had fallen into a mess because of Ivy Ann. Never again.*

The following Saturday dawned as one of the most beautiful days of summer. Laurel and Ivy Ann scorned the hopeful offers of a dozen escorts and set out for a long ride. Delicious and filling sandwiches, cookies, and two blushing peaches from some Dan Sharpe had brought rested in their saddle bags. Their canteens were full in case they chose to go up rather than down to the river or if they didn't find a stream to quench their summer thirst.

"Do you realize this will be the longest time we've had together since I got here?" Ivy Ann reined in her mount atop a low rise that afforded a view of the rolling Double B with its surrounding mountains.

"I know, it's wonderful." Laurel meant it. The new twin her sister had become didn't jangle on Laurel's nerves but offered the same companionship they'd known before

Ivy Ann discovered beaux.

"We have to stay on main trails," she warned and nudged her horse's sides with her heels.

"You won't catch me getting lost in this place," Ivy Ann said emphatically and she lifted one eyebrow. "Of course, if the right person or persons came along to rescue us —"

"You're impossible!" Laurel couldn't help laughing and thinking it wouldn't be so bad after all, provided that rescue party included Adam.

Three hours later she paid for her day-dreaming. With Laurel's hands slack on the reins as her horse stepped in a gopher hole, Laurel pitched over the horse's head and landed in a heap.

"Laurel!" Ivy Ann screamed then slid from her horse and ran to her sister. "Are you hurt?"

Laurel shook her head and spit out a mouthful of pine needles. "Ugh! I don't think so, oh, oh." She tried to stand but went down when her left ankle refused to support her. "I — I guess I sprained it." She felt her ankle gingerly. "I don't think anything's broken."

"Good." Ivy Ann pushed Laurel's hand away and gently pulled off her boot. "It's starting to swell."

Laurel's horrified gaze riveted on the ankle.

"Can you ride with it like that?"

Laurel shook her head. "You'll have to go for help."

"And leave you?" Tears streamed down her cheeks and Ivy glanced around the country that had seemed so beautiful but now appeared threatening.

"We have no choice." Laurel knew she had to be strong. "Leave me some of the sandwiches and. . . ." She broke off and stared behind Ivy Ann.

"What's wrong?" Ivy turned.

"I thought I saw something move behind that big pine but I guess there's nothing there."

Ivy Ann cast a fearful glance then bravely marched to it. "I don't see anything." She looked at the sky and noted the sun's position. "Why can't I just stay with you? Daddy will send someone."

"But not for hours," Laurel pointed out, as she bit her lip against the pain and fear falling over her like a blanket. "We told them we'd be gone all day. Hurry home and get help."

Five minutes later she watched her twin bolting down the grassy hillside and out of sight as if the devil himself pursued her.

Another few minutes passed before a familiar drawling voice cut the eerie silence. "Well, Miss Ivy Ann. I've been biding my time just waiting to cut you out of the herd. Looks like it's paid off."

Laurel twisted her body and started straight into Dan Sharpe's tiger eyes, more amber than ever in contrast to his bay horse.

"I'm not —" *Ivy Ann,* she started to say.

He didn't let her finish. "What happened?" He stepped nearer and genuine concern showed when he saw her exposed ankle. "You really messed yourself up, didn't you?" He dropped to his knees and pressed here and there.

"That hurts!" Laurel tried to pull her foot free but Dan held it fast.

"I'm on my knees to you. Isn't that what every girl wants?" Again he gave her no time to answer but sauntered to her horse. He grunted when he found the sandwiches carefully wrapped in an old napkin and transferred them to a clean rock nearby. "I'm not skilled like the Doc but wrapping it will help enough so you can ride." He deftly made a bandage and tied the ends.

"My sister has gone for help, thank you." Laurel's icy tones didn't faze him.

"Oh, we won't be going exactly the same

186

way." He shoved his hat back on his head, more predatory than ever. "I know this nice little place not far from here where we can stay, that is, until you promise to marry me."

"Marry you?" Was he totally mad? Laurel's brain seemed to explode.

"Look, Ivy Ann." He hunkered back on his boot heels. "If you're going to live out here you need a husband. The sooner the better. I've never asked a woman to marry me and I never thought I would but you aren't just any woman. First off, I fell for your sister but since getting to know you, I decided I like your spunk better." He smiled and she wanted to hit him.

"Now I'm going to get you onto your horse. Don't get any wild ideas about running away because I can catch you."

"You will be hanged for this," Laurel predicted, her tone cold and clear in spite of the hot day. "Even Antelope, wild as it is, won't allow a kidnapping."

"My dear, ignorant girl." He raised his tawny eyebrows in mock surprise. "An elopement isn't considered kidnapping even in the East, is it? I'll get you settled comfortably and go find a preacher. Sorry you can't have a church wedding and all that with the Reverend Birchfield presiding, but I know a justice of the peace who will come for certain considerations and keep his mouth shut about any story a timid bride might concoct."

Dear God, are You here? Laurel looked up with a silent cry in her heart. The same snow-topped mountains she loved reared against the same sky. Uneasy peace nudged aside some of her fears as she clung to her faith and trust in God with all her heart and soul.

Even when her lips whitened with pain as Dan lifted her into the saddle she held back tears.

"This is no good," he said as he lifted her off and laid her back on the needle-covered ground. Then he smartly slapped her horse's rump. "He will head for home," Dan said. "They'll think he broke free." He picked her up and in spite of his small stature easily carried her to the bay and mounted, cradling her so her injured foot could be supported across the saddle.

"They will track us," Laurel warned through waves of pain when he started.

"Not where we're going." He chuckled and a few minutes later when he left the soft ground and his horse's hooves clattered on rocks it took everything Laurel had to keep her from despair.

Too engrossed with carrying the injured

girl to heed his surroundings, Dan's usually keen bearing missed small, cautious sounds that warned someone pursued them. Ivy Ann had no more ridden out of sight when she realized she still carried the water canteen. Wheeling her horse back the way she had come, uneasiness filled her as she glanced around. *Why did she feel another presence? Had Laurel really seen something move?*

The thud of hooves roused Ivy and she swung her horse out of the way of the approaching steed headed straight toward her. Her eyes widened. Laurel had ridden that very horse this morning! She watched the frightened beast rush by, obviously headed for the Double B. *What had happened to terrify him like that?* she wondered.

Ivy Ann set her mouth in a straight, unyielding line. Something peculiar must be happening where she'd left Laurel and she had to know what it was. She slid from the saddle while still a short distance from the site of Laurel's accident and tied her horse to a tree, making sure the knots would hold. "Stay here and be quiet," she ordered.

Dodging behind trees Ivy sneaked back, her heart pounding from exertion, fear, and caution. Low voices reached her. A spurt of gladness vanished when she peeped out from her sheltered position. She shoved her hand over her mouth to keep back a cry.

In the clearing before her Dan Sharpe was mounting a strong bay, and he had Laurel in his arms.

"They will track us." Laurel's faint words reached her twin's straining ears.

"Not where we're going." Ivy hated Dan's laugh. Rebellion rose in a wave of protest but she sensibly stayed out of sight. *That's what you think,* she thought to herself. Her busy fingers jerked off the scarf she wore under her chin and methodically she tore it into narrow strips. "Just like in the storybooks." She grinned in spite of her worry and slipped back for her horse.

Step by careful step Ivy Ann followed the doubly burdened bay. When they reached the rocks and the horse ahead clattered on them, Ivy's hope failed. "Dear God, now what?" A few minutes later the pampered girl who must now become resourceful managed to fashion pads for her own mount's hooves of Sadie Brown's worn tablecloth.

Ivy Ann listened to make sure she was still on the right trail. The distant crack of sturdily shod hooves on rock rewarded her and she swung back into the saddle, hot and tired but filled with the most satisfaction she had ever experienced. The next instant she bowed her head. "Thank You, God. I know You helped me think what to do."

All afternoon she trailed her quarry from afar. She only caught glimpses now and then. To allow her horse to get too close to the bay could result in disaster if either whinnied.

Just when the drooping girl felt she couldn't stay in the saddle one more minute, she heard Dan Sharpe's "Whoa." Alert, she straightened and stopped her horse. Again she tied him. Again she sneaked forward and peered out from cover like ground squirrel from under a bush. Dan had dismounted and the open door of a rude shack bore witness he had reached his destination.

Ivy Ann crept closer. *If only the shack had a window!* She wormed her way around back and confronted a blank, weather-beaten solid wall. A little sob reached her throat and she backed toward the side of the cabin. Concern for Laurel overcame prudence. She stepped on a large dry pine cone and its disintegration came with a riflelike crack.

Strong hands fastened on her shoulders and whirled her around. "Who — what — ?" Dan Sharpe's mouth fell open but his grip didn't diminish.

"Hello, Dan." She jerked free in spite of the searing pain it cost her.

"Laurel? No, Ivy Ann. But —" He turned his head toward the shack. The next instant he had forced her ahead of him around the corner, onto the rotting porch and through the door of the shack.

Laurel sat on a blanketed cot, her injured ankle straight before her. Her eyes darkened when Ivy Ann burst in with Dan just behind.

"Why didn't you tell me you weren't Ivy Ann?" Dan raged. "Some more of your smart tricks?" When neither girl replied he flung his hat onto a dirty table and wiped the sweat from his forehead. His smile slowly replaced the anger in his face but its chill roused more fear in Laurel than his accusations. She glanced at Ivy who had closed her eyes, swallowed convulsively, and then opened them with a disarming expression.

"Looks like you won the jackpot, doesn't it, Dan?" Her rueful smile and the way she rubbed her aching shoulders made Laurel gasp as well as Dan. "Here we are. Now what?"

In the split second Dan's gaze left her and traveled to Laurel, Ivy glanced around the cabin for a weapon. If this were a novel an old knife should be sticking in the wall.

Even if she could find one, could she bring herself to stab Dan? She shuddered at the thought then steeled herself at the gloating in Dan's eyes when he turned back to her. Laurel couldn't help; anything done to free them must come from Ivy.

"Just what *are* your plans?" tore from her throat.

"I had planned to tie up my bride-to-be and go get a justice of the peace," Dan responded.

Horror showed in Laurel's face and in the heartbeat before Ivy Ann spoke a hundred thoughts thundered into her brain. For the first time in her life she had the chance to do something worthy. If it meant sacrificing herself to save Laurel, then she had no choice. *Dear God, give me strength.* Ivy clasped her hands in front of her in a demure pose. She glanced down then up through her lashes in the coquettish way she had done so often.

"You went to all this trouble just to marry me? Why, Dan, I'm flattered beyond belief." She forced herself to smile and look around the cabin as if considering every spider web and speck of dust. "It isn't the exact surroundings I'd have picked, but if people are in love, it doesn't matter, does it?" *All true,* she soothed her protesting conscience. Her keen gaze hesitated on the untidy stack of cut branches near the rough fireplace then turned back to Dan. He must not know her plans. She proudly lifted her chin in the best Brown manner.

"Laurel, you will be my bridesmaid, won't you?" She laughed into the two faces staring at her like white blobs and triumphed over her fear.

"No, oh no!" Laurel leaped to her feet without regard to her ankle then crumpled to the floor.

With an oath Dan sprang to lift her back onto the cot but not as quickly as Ivy Ann. With a silent cry to God for help she bounded the few steps toward the wood pile, snatched the strongest looking length of pine branch, raised it, and sent it crashing against the back of Dan Sharpe's head.

He collapsed without a single cry as Laurel fell to the cot.

THIRTEEN

Ivy Ann stood frozen to the dirty cabin floor, still clutching her weapon. A slight moan and movement showed she had not knocked Dan completely out, only stunned him. With wisdom born of prayer and desperation she ordered, "Quick, Laurel, we have to tie him."

Laurel pushed back the nausea that had risen when she jumped to her feet and ignored her throbbing ankle. "Help me tear the blanket," she cried. Four hands working as two rent the old blanket and Ivy Ann put the strips around and around Dan, tying strong knots where the pieces joined. By the time Ivy rolled him onto another cot and wound more blanket strips to pinion him exhaustion threatened her.

"You'd better look at the damage you did to his head." Laurel's faint reminder sent her twin into hysterical giggles that ended with healing tears.

"A big bump but it didn't even break the skin," Ivy said after examining Dan. She shrank back when he blinked and opened his eyes. Even in anger there had been a certain respect. Now hatred made him more dangerous than ever.

"I'll get even," he threatened. With mighty efforts he fought against his bonds. They didn't give as the twins had feared they might. But his struggles and twistings accomplished a lot more than he expected. Stubbornly refusing to admit defeat at the hands of two young women, Dan tipped over the cot and landed on the floor. The force of his fall broke the cot free from the moldy wall where it had been attached.

"Look!" Laurel pointed at the gaping hole exposed just under where the cot had come free. "A hiding place."

"Don't touch that!" Dan lost control and for the first time fear mingled with his anger.

It was too late. Ivy Ann had already grabbed the contents of the niche and carried it to the tottery table. She threw open the mouth of one of the sacks. Money spilled out. Bills, gold coins, and eventually the incriminating papers lettered *Rock Springs Bank* were all there.

"Well, Mr. Bank Robber. It looks like you'll have more to face than abducting

Laurel." Ivy Ann's contempt was thick enough to cut.

Game to the very end, Dan merely smirked. "You can't prove anything."

"You had a reason for coming to this cabin, Dan," Ivy reminded.

Dan managed a shrug in spite of his position on the floor. He shifted his weight and growled. "Help me up, will you?"

It took all Ivy Ann's remaining gumption to right the cot then she faced him squarely. "Dan, if Laurel and I tell the ranchers what you tried to do today they'll hang you." She shuddered and some of her fearlessness left. "If you confess to the bank robbery it will mean prison but not death. Which do you choose?"

Dan's jaw dropped in amazement. A flicker of something neither twin had ever seen in him surfaced into his eyes. "You mean you'll say nothing if I admit to the robbery?"

Ivy Ann turned to Laurel who nodded. "You have our word."

"But why?" Dull red marred the skin, the red of shame before such generosity. "I'd think you —"

Ivy took a long, deep breath. "If this had happened a few months ago in West Virginia only Laurel would have spared you. After she left, and especially since I came out here, I've learned that a child of God cannot harbor hatred, no matter what." She spread her hands wide. "Dan, letting you off even when I boil inside to think how you might have actually forced Laurel into marriage —" She choked then determinedly went on. "It's for my sake as well as yours." Understanding lit up her face. "No, it isn't! It's for Jesus' sake."

An indiscernible murmur came from Dan. He ceased fighting and sagged against the blanket ropes. "You sound just like Preacher Birchfield." Astonishment still filled his face. "You and he would make a real pair."

Ivy Ann couldn't keep the hot color from her cheeks. If she had been honest, she'd have retorted, "I think so, too," but pride sealed her lips.

Laurel's anxious reminder switched her thoughts back to the present and away from some vague future possibility. "What are we going to do now?"

Ivy Ann looked at her then at Dan. With a lithe movement she stepped closer to the old cot and looked down on him. "If I untie you will you give me your word of honor you won't try to run or hold us here in any way? That you will confess you robbed the Rock Springs bank?"

"Ivy!"

Laurel's shocked cry didn't change her twin. "Will you?" she repeated.

The tawny eyes blinked. "You'd take my word for it?"

"If you swear to do what I say." She staked her claim on the good Thomas Brown had taught her was in every man, often hidden but there.

"I swear." The husky words brought relief to Ivy's tense body.

"Do you have a knife?"

"In my belt." Dan acted dazed by the turn of events.

"We made them pretty tight," Ivy matter-of-factly stated as she began hacking away at the confining strips. When she finished, she felt relief at having come through the ordeal without real harm and a fervent prayer left Ivy's heart. One day, with God's help, Dan Sharpe might accept Jesus and leave the life he had embraced in this wild country.

Ivy dropped into an old chair. "Now all we have to do is wait until help comes." She stared out the open door, dreading the night that must pass before a rescue party arrived.

Some of Dan's sardonic humor remained. "No rescue party can find this place. Remember all the rocks we came over?" He looked down at his hands, still showing faint red streaks where Ivy had imprisoned him tightly.

"Oh, they'll come. I dropped pieces of my scarf all along the way," she told him confidently.

"Well, I'll be!" Dan threw back his head in the same way as Nat and Adam Birchfield. His laughter rang through the little cabin and the twins couldn't help joining in. Bank robber, would-be bridegroom, and rascal he might be, but that clean laugh brought back pleasant memories when he had squired first Laurel and then Ivy Ann.

Long after Ivy Ann had served a sandwich supper supplemented by the few stores in the shack, a naughty wind wakened, came to life, and howled its protest for miles around. It left only after greedily claiming the torn scarf markers Ivy Ann had so carefully left on the trail.

All day Adam had been restless. For some unexplainable reason few patients claimed his time and by late afternoon he restlessly paced the floor of his small office.

"What's troubling you?"

Nat's voice from the open doorway stopped Adam. "Just thinking. Probably too much." He took another turn.

"About Laurel Brown." Nat's dark eyes offered sympathy.

Adam stared unseeingly out the window then glanced back at Nat. "Why didn't she tell me? You've been with her lately." He hoped Nat hadn't caught the bitterness in his tone.

"I've thought about it even though she hasn't told me any more than you know," Nat confided.

Adam's heart beat faster. Relief nudged aside his still smoldering resentment at being made to look like a fool. Nat didn't sound as if he had fallen in love with Laurel.

Nat's fine features clouded. "Perhaps much of it goes back to always being in her sister's shadow." His gaze met his brother's frowning look. "Remember, she never — according to you — claimed to be Ivy Ann. You just assumed it."

"But she should have told me when I told her I — I — when we discussed certain things," Adam protested. Fresh disappointment pressed heavily into his soul. "She didn't lie but her silence consented to the deception."

"The one thing she ever said that gave me a clue was simply to relate what you once told her about hating deception more than anything on earth." Nat stepped inside, closed the door, and spoke boldly. "I believe Laurel cared so much for you that she followed you out here, felt cut to the heart when you mistook her for Ivy Ann, and grew terrified that you'd despise her when you learned the truth. I also think she hoped you would grow so close you could forgive her once she found the courage to confess."

Adam listened silently, wanting to believe.

"I don't want to preach, but how many times has our Heavenly Father forgiven us when we've stumbled and been afraid or when we've made bad decisions?" For a moment his mouth twisted. "Adam, don't ever be like Father, miserable in Concord with his two sons thousands of miles away because of his unforgiving spirit." He laid one hand on his brother's shoulder and Adam felt he'd been given a blessing.

"Thanks, old man." His hand clasped Nat's. To break the quivering moment he added, "I've been coming to that conclusion. Just one thing." He paused and tightened his hold on Nat's hand. "Do you care about Laurel?"

"Very much." Mischief sparkled in Nat's dark eyes. "But I'm not in love with her. Someday, God and Ivy Ann willing, we may be brothers-in-law as well as brothers!"

A knock on the outside office door came

simultaneously and Dr. Adam Birchfield found himself extremely busy for the next few hours.

Dark had encroached when a loud knocking sent Adam and Nat both to the door. Thomas Brown strode in without waiting for an invitation. His agitation showed with every jerky sentence.

"The twins didn't come home. We didn't think anything at first. They'd planned to spend the day and they know the country as far as they were going. Then Laurel's horse came in just a little bit ago. The boys rode out but it's too dark to find out anything. They're still out and we thought it would be good to have you at the ranch — both of you — just in case. . . ." His voice trailed off.

Nat and Adam sprang to attention and a few minutes later pounded down the pale moonlit road behind Thomas. Adam longed to leave the others and plunge off to the rescue but he restrained himself. He didn't know the country as well as those already searching, and if, no, *when,* the twins came in he must be at the Double B.

One by one the groups returned. Lanterns bobbed from horses' backs in a weird yellow glow that competed with the feeble moonlight. Rising wind and dancing shadows made searching impossible until morning. Somehow they lived through it, the Browns who had faced and conquered similar fears all during the War Between the States, the Birchfields, bonded closer than ever by their love for Laurel and Ivy Ann. Now and then one attempted to reassure the others by commenting on how trailwise the twins had become. For the most part, each kept a silent and prayerful vigil and thanked God the night stayed warm despite the screeching wind.

"At least there's two of them," said Hardwick, who had come immediately when summoned by one of the Double B hands. "We'll find them in the morning all curled up together and just waiting for us to bring breakfast."

But his prophecy was doomed from the start. Before morning the wind changed to rain and washed out the tracks needed to follow the twins.

Adam impatiently waited for dawn's gray light with a prayer for his own stubbornness following his petitions to God to be with them. First to be ready and mounted, he looked down in disbelief when pale but calm Nat stopped him from heading out in the direction the twins had first taken the morning before.

"Adam, you can't do a thing the hands can't."

Protest rose in his throat and denial but Nat never let him speak.

"Listen, the only one I know who might still find some sign after the rain is Chief Grey Eagle or Running Deer. Ride as fast as you can and ask for their help. They will never forget their debt to you for saving Running Deer." He gripped Adam's hand. "Ride as if life depended on it but still use care in the high and treacherous places."

Adam never remembered much of his ride to the Indian village. Filled with fear and worry, he scarcely saw the trail except as a hurdle that must be leaped so Laurel and Ivy Ann could be saved.

Cries of gladness greeted his arrival. He sprang from the back of his sweaty horse to greet his friends. All looked well and he rejoiced at the way Chief Grey Eagle's dead black eyes lighted. He quickly sketched the crisis: the lost young women, the wind and rain, the loss of all tracks.

"Running Deer will go." Grey Eagle gestured and in moments fresh horses stood ready. "Grey Eagle's eyes grow old but his son's are new like the morning."

"Thank you." Adam blinked hard. Not a question, not a second of hesitation, just the sending of his son. How like another Father who sent His Son to help save the lost!

He silently shook hands with Chief Grey Eagle, nodded to his old friend the medicine man and the others, then sprang to the back of the now-saddled Indian pony and rode away, humbled by the depths of gratitude in the hidden tribe.

Ivy Ann awakened from her uncomfortable bed on the floor beside the fireplace to the steady drum of rain. She rubbed sleep from her eyes and stole glances at Dan and Laurel, still asleep on the rickety cots. Dan had been furious when she insisted on making a nest of old blankets and a saddle blanket for herself. "You think I'm going to sleep on the cot and let you huddle there?" He staggered a little but fiercely glared at her.

"Dan, I don't like the way your face is flushed," she told him. "I'll be fine. You have to rest." She observed again the dull color in his cheeks and his listless eyes that showed even an inexperienced nurse such as herself the presence of a low-grade fever. Only when he tried to get up and fell back from sheer weakness did Dan stop arguing.

He looked cooler this morning and Laurel's tousled light brown curls spilled over the coarse blanket in utter relaxation. At least Ivy Ann wouldn't have two patients here in this forsaken shack.

She thought of Dan's full confession the night before. His freighting in of supplies had won the confidence of those he bought from and sold to. One day he'd noticed how the Rock Springs banker carelessly left his keys on the desk while talking with Dan. A niggling idea grew. The next time Dan went to see the banker he carried a lump of soft clay in his pocket. This time the keys didn't appear but several visits later they did and when his banker acquaintance was called away for a few minutes, Dan made an impression. Later he constructed a crude key and polished it. Then one night he stole down a dark street, used his key, and helped himself. At first he secreted the money in the bottom of his wagon. When he heard of the deserted trapper's cabin he painstakingly gouged out a cache in the wall, covered by the cot.

"Why, Dan?" Ivy Ann had burst out.

He shrugged. "I always wanted a cattle ranch but never could afford one."

"And now?" Laurel's soft voice accused him as her sister's had done.

Dan's brittle laugh little resembled his

earlier honest mirth. "Prison. A long stretch." He yawned and Ivy Ann saw his hand tremble. Then Dan closed his eyes and the twins sat silently. A little later, all three slept.

All that day they waited for someone to come. Dan never fell unconscious or grew delirious but Ivy Ann wouldn't let him ride out for help.

"Are you afraid I won't keep my word?" he challenged.

Surprise underlined every word. "Of course not. You just aren't in any condition to ride." One dimple showed as she couldn't resist saying, "Look, Mr. Sharpe. We're keeping still about something that could end with you dead. I'm not going to let you ride out of here, fall off your horse, and lie somewhere hurt. It wouldn't do any of us the least bit of good."

He subsided, too tired to care. "You sure pack a mean wallop." He gingerly rubbed the goose egg on the back of his head. "I'm sorry you had to do it," he mumbled.

"So am I," Ivy Ann quietly told him. Then she gathered up the rag ropes and burned them.

Ivy Ann managed to clean up the shack a bit and, by using a few more of the old stores, get a creditable meal. "Good thing we always pack a lot more than food than we need," she said. They ate and she scrubbed the battered tin dishes she'd had to wash in boiling water before using.

Evening melted into dusk. Now nothing remained except to wait.

FOURTEEN

Wait. The most difficult word in the English language, Adam thought. He stared into the curtain of rain just outside the rude shelter of boughs Running Deer had constructed when a downpour caught the two on their way back to the Double B. *What went on in his companion's mind behind the dark eyes that betrayed nothing?* Running Deer seldom spoke, and, when he did, only in response to Adam's direct questions. Yet in the space of an hour the Indian, with Adam's less skilled help, had found dry roots in spite of the cloudburst, built a roaring fire, and provided shelter.

Could he have done as well? Adam wondered. Probably not. He still had a lot to learn about survival in the Wyoming Territory. *You still have a lot to learn about forgiveness, too,* a voice inside prodded. The memory of Laurel's expression haunted him. He had originally considered it triumphant that her little joke had gone on so long. Now he knew it for pleading. If she cared as Nat felt sure, the hurt must have gone deep.

By the time the rain let up enough for Adam and Running Deer to reach the ranchhouse then follow to the spot where Nat led them to the rest of the rescue party, despair filled Adam. No one could find a sign after the rain, not even Running Deer. "How do you know they were ever here?" he asked Hardwick, who slouched low in his saddle, his hat brim down and collar turned up against the weather.

"Found tracks we recognized under a tree where the rain hadn't soaked through." Hardwick's terse reply warmed Adam but he chilled again when Hardwick continued. "Found somethin' else, too." His keen eyes bored into Adam. "You said the twins rode out alone?"

"That's right," Thomas broke in. The hours since his daughters failed to ride in had aged him.

"Well, they weren't alone all the time."

With a southerner's quickness to take offense, Thomas drew himself up and his voice turned icy. "What are you implying, sir? That my daughters planned to meet someone here?"

"Simmer down," Hardwick told the irate father. "I'm just sayin' we found tracks of three different horses." His voice softened. "Look, Tom, no one in this country would believe anythin' bad about your girls. It appears some galoot came along and —"

A call from Running Deer a little to one side of the clearing interrupted Hardwick's speculations. Adam, Nat, and the others hurried to him. The Indian silently held out a sodden bit of color-dulled cloth.

"Why, that looks like the scarf Ivy Ann wears so much." Thomas Brown reached for it.

A rare, slow smile crossed Running Deer's unreadable face.

"Where did you find it?" Hope flared in Adam's chest.

Running Deer pointed to a nearby clump of trees and Adam reached them in one leap, closely followed by Nat. Yet a thorough search disclosed no more clues.

"Spread out and search every inch of ground," Hardwick ordered. Adam stuck with Running Deer. Nat joined Samuel. The hands paired up and agreed to meet again in an hour or to fire three shots if they discovered anything more.

For the second time that day Adam realized how far short his newly acquired woodcraft fell compared with Running Deer's skills. If the situation hadn't been so terrifying in its unknown possibilities, Adam would have rejoiced in the education he received in noticing seemingly trivial things. Running Deer left no area until he had examined the smallest patches of ground. Even when their steps clattered on rock, the tracker's intent scrutiny checked out each broken branch or overturned stone. Fifteen minutes later he dug a second bit of torn cloth from under the edge of a dislodged rock.

"Running Deer, you are a wonder!" Adam burst out in admiration. He fired into the air three times to summon the others, excitement sending relief through his tense body. But when the rescue party re-assembled, to their dismay two other pairs had also found bits of scarf!

"Wind blow hard." Running Deer's sweeping gesture told the sad story. Then he turned back to his search, closely followed by a discouraged Adam.

It felt like a month later when the tracker's pleased grunt brought Adam out of his misery to stare at a track in the softer earth alongside the rocky path. Deep, partly filled with rainwater, it offered a spurt of hope.

Hardwick pushed his hat back from his

grimy forehead and his eyes glistened. "Isn't there some kind of old tumbledown shack back a ways from here?"

The Indian straightened from measuring the track with his open palm. "Pony carry two. Make heavy track."

Again Adam's spirits dragged in the muddy earth. He saw Nat's concern, heard Thomas gasp, and noticed the way the searchers shifted uneasily from one foot to the other. If the horse that made the track carried two persons, one must be hurt. Hardwick's observation about three horses plus the return of Laurel's horse could mean just one thing and Adam didn't want to consider it. *Maybe not,* he told himself. Perhaps someone came along and offered assistance because the twins only had one horse between them. On the other hand, why would a Good Samaritan of the mountains head toward some obscure hut miles away from Antelope instead of going back to the Double B?

A frantic prayer for their safety sprang from Adam's trembling heart and he silently followed Running Deer, who methodically continued his tracking.

Darkness descended before they reached the long-forsaken and overgrown trail Hardwick vaguely remembered might lead to the shack. A few more bits of scarf in such a fantastically scattered pattern helped little. Running Deer's discovery of a few more tracks and his statement that "one pony go, one follow" dished up speculation while the men drank hot coffee and ate the steaming supper Hardwick handily prepared.

Hardwick's persuasive voice and bright eyes in the firelit circle of rescuers splashed into a little pool of silence. "The way I figure it is, whoever's ridin' that second horse is the one who kept droppin' those little bitty pieces of scarf. Maybe they were tied and came off in the wind. Or maybe the person leavin' the trail didn't count on a storm."

"But what's it supposed to mean if that *is* what happened?" Thomas wanted to know. His hands gripped his tin cup until they resembled claws.

"I'd say someone —" Hardwick paused and Adam's nerves silently screamed for him to continue.

"Someone for some reason and none of us knows why must have put one of the twins on his horse and the other moseyed along behind leavin' signs for whoever came when Laurel's horse got home." Hardwick raised his coffee cup in tribute and silently drank to the resourcefulness of a tenderfoot woman smart enough not to panic but to leave evidence of her pursuit.

Hours later Nat stirred beside a wide-eyed Adam. "Are you asleep?"

"No."

The strong hand that used to comfort a small boy now gripped Adam's. "We may not know where they are but God does."

"I know." Yet dread never left Adam's heart and mind. He shifted on his pine-needle bed. "Nat, sometimes God lets things happen. Even to those who love and serve Him."

"And sometimes He doesn't." The big hand squeezed harder. "Remember what Jesus said? 'Where two or three are gathered together in my name, there am I in the midst of them.'* I'll bet there isn't a man here tonight — including Running Deer who prays to the Great Spirit — who isn't thinking of and praying for them."

Strangely calmed, his faith bolstered by the unshakable tone in his older brother's voice, Adam clasped Nat's hand until his own ached and a little later fell into an uneasy sleep. He awoke to a fiery, red-streaked sky that made Hardwick mutter. The search party gulped hot coffee and ate

* Matthew 18:20 (KJV)

216

meat slapped into cold biscuits as they traveled behind Running Deer into a world where faces, rocks, and even trees reflected the awe-inspiring heavens. Deeper into the mountains they went, buoyed by Running Deer's steady progress and infrequent pointing to tracks. The red in the sky died. Gray-black clouds roiled and gathered. Running Deer stopped dead still and sniffed the air.

"By the powers, *smoke!*" Hardwick gave an exultant yell. Running Deer's rare smile came once more and he bounded down a little corridor made where branches along the little-used trail had been broken by the passage of animals. Minutes later the little group rounded a bend. Before them stood a rotting shack. Moss splotched the roof but from a crooked tin pipe came a white wisp of smoke.

"Laurel? Ivy Ann?" Thomas pushed aside the others and ran to the weathered door of the dirty cabin with his rescue party close behind. Without stopping to knock or use the caution Hardwick would have advised, Thomas Brown crashed open the door.

"Daddy!" A woman with a soot-stained face from trying to heat water in the decrepit fireplace rose and flung herself into her father's arms.

Adam looked past the twin he knew was Ivy Ann, but a changed Ivy Ann with a look of maturity he'd never seen in her face. Laurel sat propped on a blanketed cot, her bandaged ankle straight out in front of her. Her pinched face had never been more beautiful to Adam. He crossed the small room with giant strides and loomed over her. "Laurel, my darling, are you all right?"

Bright tears gathered. So did color more glowing than the morning's sky. "I hurt my ankle. Mr. Sharpe, Ivy Ann, we came here and —" she faltered.

Dan Sharpe shrugged his shoulders, the flush of fever dulling his eyes but not his audacity. "I might as well 'fess up. The girls just captured themselves a bank robber." He pointed to the sacks on the rickety table, still gaping open and spilling out incriminating evidence. A ripple of shock filled the cabin.

The doctor in Adam took over. He marched to the second cot and examined Dan's head. "How did you do this?"

Dan's mouth twitched. "Took a bad fall." His eyes laughed.

"Is that right, Laurel? Ivy Ann?" Adam looked from one to the other. Something about the whole thing didn't feel right.

"He took a terrible fall," Ivy confirmed

from the depths of her father's embrace. "I wouldn't let him ride for help."

"That's right," Laurel told the stunned group. "We made him swear he'd confess the robbery. He gave his word."

Hardwick said heavily, "He may be a robber but I never knew Dan Sharpe to go back on his word." He sent a piercing glance at Ivy Ann. "I reckon 'twas you who rode the horse that followed the first one. Why'd you leave pieces of your scarf?"

"I wasn't sure I could find my way back out of here," she admitted. "You see, I'd started back for help after Laurel got hurt. Then I went back to leave the canteen with her and saw Laurel's horse heading for home." She paused. "Anyway, Dan had come along and found Laurel hurt so I came after them." She rushed on. "We got here and Dan fell and I've been taking care of them and praying for someone to come." She looked up into Nathaniel Birchfield's face and something passed between them, something to be taken out and examined when the present crisis became nothing but an adventuresome memory.

"If it hadn't been for Running Deer you'd have been here a lot longer," Nat said soberly. With one accord they turned toward the open doorway.

"Why, where is he?" Adam left Laurel and raced back out the shabby door. Only the grumble of thunder in the distance and a few large rain drops spattering on the ground greeted him. "Running Deer?" Adam cupped his hands around his mouth. *"Running Deer!"*

A rough hand that still held kindness fell on Adam's shoulder. "It's no use, son. He's gone." Hardwick lowered his voice. "He did what Chief Grey Eagle sent him to do."

"I didn't even thank him."

"The way I hear tell you did that a long time ago when you and that brother of yours went to a certain hidden village and you saved Running Deer's life just like you saved my wife's."

"How did you know?" Adam whirled. "We promised not to betray the location of the tribe."

"Son, this is my country and I pretty much know what's happenin'." Hardwick grinned but his steady look never wavered. "I'm also known for keepin' my mouth shut, so don't worry none. Now come back inside. We've got to decide whether to make a run for it or stay here tonight." He glanced at the storm-laden sky. "I person'ly vote for stayin'. The horses are tired and it will give the girls and Dan a little extra time." He sighed and his good humor faded. "Sure hate to find out Dan Sharpe's a thief. He's gotta be punished and they'll give him a lot of time for this. Maybe since he surrendered nice and gentlemanlike, and since everyone will get their money back, the judge won't go too hard on him."

Later that night when the newcomers disposed of themselves as well as they could on the floor and were joined by Dan who refused to let Ivy Ann sleep on the floor again, Adam heard Hardwick whispering. He strained his ears to hear.

"Sharpe, if I thought there was more to all this than the girls are tellin' I'd horsewhip you 'til there wasn't enough left for a trial."

Adam's heart skipped a beat when Dan retorted half under his breath, "Go to the devil, Hardwick. Are you questioning the word of two finest girls that ever hit the Wyoming Territory, or anywhere else?"

Hardwick grunted and subsided. Adam lay awake to marvel. Rogue, rascal, and bank robber, Dan Sharpe still recognized and bowed before the simple goodness of Christian women. How right Nat had been about the need for such women in this wild place! How many would-be Dans remained for the Brown twins and others to influence, to catch before they turned to crime and wickedness?

He thought of Mark Justice who continued to baffle his pards by accepting Jesus Christ. One or two even came to church with Mark occasionally. God grant that the tiny seeds being dropped along the way, as Ivy Ann had dropped pieces of her scarf, would take root and not be blown away with the first wind that came.

For another day and night the new fall storm imprisoned the group. The cowboys made no attempt to hide their admiration for the plucky twins or their disgust for Dan, the fallen. Thomas beamed and lamented, "If only Sadie could know everything's all right!"

Hardwick offered the opinion that Running Deer would stop at the Double B before heading home. Adam couldn't keep himself from staring at Laurel and checking her ankle often merely to be close to her. Nat and Ivy Ann exchanged furtive glances that brought color to both faces and warmth to Adam's soul.

Pale sun greeted the new day. A weary band of riders swept into the Double B in late afternoon. Laurel and Ivy Ann waved goodbye to Nat, Adam, and Hardwick who officially escorted Dan Sharpe back to Antelope and to jail. Limping inside, they bathed and fell into their beds.

Laurel woke first. Ivy Ann lay in the abandonment of deep sleep, her arms spread wide like a broken doll's. Laurel studied her twin's face. A new set to Ivy's red lips showed the results of taking responsibility and facing fear.

Laurel stretched and slid deeper into her quilts. Her ankle barely twinged. Now she had time to take out of hiding the look Adam bestowed on her when he followed Thomas into the shack and the timbre of his voice when he called her darling. Instead of the censure she had learned to expect, forgiveness and something more made her heart pound and her pulse race even harder than that awful moment when Ivy Ann struck Dan and he tumbled to the floor.

"Laurel?" Ivy Ann sat bolt upright in bed. Her cambric nightgown rose and fell with her breathing. Hair tousled and face flushed, the new love and concern in her face touched Laurel deeply. "Are you really, truly all right?"

Sheer happiness spilled into laughter and Laurel stretched.

"Thanks to God and Adam and Running Deer and the rest, I'm really, truly all right."

"You left out Nat!" Ivy Ann protested.

"I wouldn't want to do that," Laurel

teased and caught the telltale color in Ivy's face. She propped herself up on one elbow and rested her chin in her hand. "You'd better not, either. I have a strong feeling Nathaniel Birchfield isn't about to let himself be left out, especially when it comes to one Ivy Ann Brown."

"You really think so?" Could this be the remote, heartless twin who had delighted in collecting and discarding beaux the way children do dandelions?

Ivy Ann interlaced her fingers and stared at her sister with a new humility. "If he doesn't love me I'll — I'll —"

"Not die. Only heroines in novels languish away, not pioneer young women in the Wyoming Territory."

"Of all the callous individuals! Never in all my born days did I expect that my own twin sister would be so unsympathetic." Ivy Ann snatched her lacy pillow and fired it at Laurel with some of her old imperiousness. But the next moment she sank back into a little heap and stared at Laurel from tragic dark eyes. "If you had any feeling in you at all you'd know the very idea Nat may still think I could never make a good minister's wife leaves me sick and so scared I don't know what to do." She sighed and stared. "I wonder how long it will take me to show him I've changed?" She didn't seem to notice how Laurel flinched.

FIFTEEN

Dan Sharpe received a sentence of twenty years of hard labor in prison for robbing the Rock Springs bank. The town of Antelope buzzed with the men upholding the sentence and many of the girls and women were secretly regretful that "such a pleasant, courteous young man" could be so wicked. Sally Mae Justice and others Dan had never deigned to notice sighed at the loss of an eligible man they had considered a little above the cowboys who called on them.

Laurel and Ivy Ann, no worse for their escapade but far more careful, soon rode out again and marveled at the coming of autumn. Nights grew crisp. Skies took on blue tones that provided a perfect backdrop for golden aspen and cottonwood leaves by day and giant, white stars by night. Along with their new neighbors, the Browns canned and dried and pickled for the coming winter. Distant peaks, then those nearer, accepted their white winter coats while bears stuffed themselves to prepare for hibernation and squirrels and chipmunks gathered nuts and seeds and acorns against the inevitable cold.

Adam and Nat had long since visited the Indian village with packhorse loads of supplies to help Chief Grey Eagle and his people through the winter should they be snowed in and without adequate food. Their thanks to Running Deer had been brushed aside but his rare smile showed his pleasure at their visit. On that trip Nat broached the subject of bringing the twins to see the village.

"Are women your wives?" Chief Grey Eagle demanded.

Adam and Nat looked at each other and grinned. "Not yet but we hope soon," Nat confessed and dug his toe in the ground like a small boy caught in mischief. Adam wanted to laugh.

"Will betray Chief Grey Eagle's nest?"

"No, Chief. Laurel and Ivy Ann know how to keep secrets." Adam's heart added, *and how!*

"You bring them. Soon, before snow comes."

The following Saturday Nat and Ivy Ann and Adam and Laurel rode out from the

Double B the way they had done many times. No one paid any particular attention except one of the cowboys perched on the rail of the coral. "Wish I had a purty gal to ride with instead of bein' a pore, lonesome cowpoke." His grin flashed white. "Maybe I shoulda been a doc or a preacher." He scratched his head when everyone laughed.

"I don't see nothin' funny but then I'm just a —"

"Pore, lonesome cowboy," Ivy and Laurel finished for him.

They rode away from his good-natured complaining into the happiness only the young and in love can know on a western Wyoming autumn day.

Adam suddenly realized something that had been nibbling at him for several weeks. "You don't dress alike any more, do you?" He glanced from Laurel to Ivy Ann and back.

Laurel's long lashes hid her eyes as she sounded demure. "We're afraid someone might take us for each other and we can't chance that." She looked up and smiled.

Adam casually added, "Good idea. It can save a heap of trouble, as Hardwick says." The minute the words left his mouth he regretted them. Laurel's face turned scarlet and her smile faded. *How sensitive she was,* he thought. A protective wave of love flowed through Adam and he reined in his horse. "Laurel, there's something I must say to you."

"I know." It came out as barely a whisper but she courageously raised her head and looked directly into his eyes. "Before you do, I want you to know I really meant to tell you I wasn't Ivy Ann." The words rushed out like the gurgling brook back home. "I had promised myself that the very next time you called I would confess but then Ivy Ann came. I had waited too long." Her lips trembled. "My only excuse is that I couldn't bear for you to think badly of me." She seemed to droop in the saddle.

The last trace of lingering resentment fled forever. Adam dismounted more rapidly than ever before, reached up both hands, and helped Laurel to the ground. But instead of releasing her, he put his hands on her shoulders and drew her close. "I've been mule-stubborn and unforgiving and for the rest of my life I'll regret it," he told her. "Laurel, a long time ago I told you how love came without my realizing it when I first saw you on the porch of Red Cedars in your blue dress." He saw hope spring to her dark eyes and tenderly pulled her unresisting form so close her head rested against his chest just under his chin.

"If you think you can forgive me, Miss Mountain Laurel Brown, I'd like to ask your father for your hand in marriage." The format proposal in all its foolishness covered his rapidly beating heart but he knew she would understand.

Laurel started to reply but Adam gently laid his fingers across her mouth. "Before you answer, you need to know I'll never live anywhere except Antelope, unless of course God calls me to another place. Once you said you would be like Ruth and follow your man where God led. Do you still feel the same way?"

Adam, the mountains, and the sky waited for her response. Even the slight breeze that lifted the light brown curls from her temples hesitated for a moment.

" 'Whither thou goest. . . .' " Laurel's whisper came only to Adam's waiting heart and ears, so low he strained to hear her, yet shouting the wondrous news of her love. He tipped her head back and kissed her. Her arms went up and around his neck and tightened. Like a frightened baby bird that has been returned to its nest, she clung to his strength. Whatever life in this still-primitive land held could not defeat her with Adam as her husband, lover, and shield.

A long time later they remounted, their faces glowing with love and reflecting the holy moments when they had knelt together and dedicated their coming oneness to the service of their Lord. Nat and Ivy Ann had no need to ask why the other couple had lingered far behind. When Adam and Laurel finally caught up with them before they entered the hidden Indian village, their entwined hands gave them away.

"You're *engaged!*" Ivy Ann blurted out the instant she saw them.

"Yes, and we're going to be married just as soon as we can." Adam flung his head back. "I've waited too long already. Late October or at least the very first of November we'll be giving you some business, parson."

Nat's dark eyes twinkled. "I'll be ready." He turned to Ivy Ann and a tiny pulse beat in his throat. "Seeing as how you're twins and all, how about making it a double wedding, Ivy Ann?"

Her laughter died. Her face paled until her eyes looked enormous and she cast a frantic glance toward Laurel. *Surely Nathaniel wouldn't joke about such a sacred thing as marriage,* she thought. Yet when she glanced back she could read little in his lean face. To cover the hot tears crowding behind her eye, she flared, "How — how could you, Nat Birchfield? I hate you!" She touched her heels to her horse and pelted down the trail.

"For mercy's sake, stop her," Laurel cried. Adam headed after Ivy but Nat sat on his horse, shocked and bewildered.

"What did I do? I thought taking her by surprise might give me an advantage." His troubled gaze turned from the two racing figures back to Laurel.

"Have you ever once told her that you love her?" Laurel demanded, torn between fear for her twin's physical safety and annoyance with Nat, whom she adored.

Misery crept into his face and settled it into lines that made him look far older than his years. "I thought at the cabin that perhaps she cared but I couldn't be sure, and —"

Compassion blotted out irritation. "Nat, Ivy Ann loves you more than life, just as I love Adam." The words sent a thrill through Laurel's heart. "She has changed so much and for weeks has feared you would only see in her the shallow person she used to be." This was no time for more misunderstanding but a time to fight for her sister's happiness. "Mama told me the minute I left she saw a change in Ivy Ann. She will make a wonderful minister's wife. We've talked how there will be times you cannot share with her those private confessions from your people's lives. She knows and accepts this." Laurel slapped her mount's neck with the reins to get him moving.

"I guess I don't know much about women." He soberly clucked to his horse and followed Laurel. "I've even wondered if the age difference is too much."

"It would have been in West Virginia, but not out here." Laurel relented and gave Nat a dazzling smile. "Get things made up with Ivy Ann as soon as you can, brother."

His old audacity that added charm but never detracted from his vocation brought a sparkle back to Nat. "I will."

By the time they reached the next cluster of trees Adam had overtaken and slowed Ivy Ann. She sat proudly, chin high, and stared straight ahead.

Nat slid from his horse in one fluid motion that reminded Laurel of Adam and marched over to the now-flushed girl. "Ivy Ann, I —"

"Do you want us to go ahead?" Adam interrupted.

A violent shake of Nat's head preceded

his simple declaration of love. "Ivy Ann, you're all I ever dreamed of in a woman during my long, lonely years of wandering. I love you and always will. Do you think an old bachelor like me can make you happy?"

Laurel felt she had glimpsed heaven when she saw the look in Ivy's face, a look that matched her own soul at the moment Adam had asked her to be his wife. "Come." Laurel held out one hand to Adam and they quietly rode on, confident that Nat and Ivy Ann never knew when they left.

A poignant moment came when the Birchfield men introduced Laurel and Ivy Ann to Chief Grey Eagle and his people. The erect old man looked at one then the other. "It is good. Always there will be friendship between Grey Eagle and you." The two couples left the Indian village bathed in afternoon sunlight, feeling they had been given a blessing of peace.

That night after the excitement and rejoicing over the two engagements, Ivy Ann and Laurel huddled close whispering secrets. Once Laurel hesitated then nodded. Once Ivy Ann raised her voice then quickly lowered it. The next day a cryptic message left Antelope and sped on its way.

The twins didn't care about a big wedding but soon realized they couldn't avoid one. When Thomas and Sadie, Widow Terry and Mrs. Greer, and the Hardwicks pointed out how the town and range felt a certain ownership in their doctor and minister and would feel slighted if left out, the twins gracefully gave in. On the first of November the sweet-smelling pine log church would be smothered with the outdoors. Dozens of willing hands would bring in scarlet leaves, still-green vines, and whatever else they could find for decoration. Ivy Ann blinked wet eyes when Nat proudly led her to the cabin Antelope had raised for their new home so Adam and Laurel could have Nat's former cabin that now included Adam's office.

"They keep bringing us things I know they can't really afford to give," Ivy protested, as she laid her hand on a gorgeous patchwork quilt. "Why, Mrs. Terry could have made several dresses in the time she took to make ours and it was all Mama could do to convince her the bride's parents must at least pay for the heavy silk!"

"I know, but Adam says they feel they can't afford *not* to give." Laurel stroked the frame of a fresh painting Mr. Hardwick had dropped off just that morning. It pictured a valley at sunrise. Molten silver edged the clouds and with the skill of a true artist,

Mrs. Hardwick had painted a feeling of peace in the rolling hills and mighty, watching mountains the twins had come to love. "Real giving comes from the heart."

"I hope *our* present comes in time." Ivy Ann broached the thought Laurel carried constantly.

"So do I but there isn't much time left."

The double wedding day outdid itself. " 'Happy is the bride the sun shines on,' " Ivy Ann caroled while she and Laurel hurriedly dressed. "Come on, Laurel. We have to give our present to Nat and Adam before the wedding." She giggled. "Doesn't Antelope frown that those eastern girls are taking such a chance on bad luck by actually letting their husbands-to-be see them on their wedding day before the wedding?"

"Who cares?" Laurel's exhilaration matched Ivy Ann's at her wildest. "God is in charge of these weddings, not superstition." She exchanged a secret glance with her twin. "I can't wait to see Adam and Nat's faces when —"

"Ivy, Laurel, your young men are here! Come down for breakfast right now."

Too happy even to laugh over their mother's orders, the twins bounced downstairs and demurely took their places at the table.

"Can you believe they are sitting there stuffing themselves?" Adam demanded of Nat. "I thought brides got so nervous they didn't eat and sometimes passed out during the ceremony."

Nat lifted arched eyebrows. "Let them eat. It will save us embarrassment at the town covered-dish dinner. They'll be too full to disgrace their new husbands by displaying such wholesome appetites."

"I notice neither of you is turning down extra biscuits," said Ivy Ann as she calmly reached for another. So did Laurel.

"Hey, that's different!" The whole family broke into laughter at Adam's involuntary protest.

"Run along, children," Sadie admonished them, but she gave the twins a stern stare. "Mind that you be back here by eleven o'clock. It takes time for brides to dress and I won't have it said my girls were late to their own wedding." She turned to Nat. "Did your minister friend from Rock Springs get here?"

He nodded. "Yesterday afternoon. Right after I pronounce Adam and Laurel husband and wife I'll step down and stand next to Ivy Ann for our turn." He beamed and she blushed becomingly.

An hour later the two happy couples

reined in at the top of the rise that over-looked Antelope. Laurel looked at Ivy Ann who then nodded as she took a deep breath. "We have a very special present for you. It's from both of us to both of you."

"I thought getting you was present enough," Adam teased.

She felt delicate color rise from her high collar but chose to ignore his comment. Instead she reached into the pocket of her riding skirt and drew out an envelope.

Adam and Nat looked apprehensive. Nat protested, "You aren't giving us money, are you? We agreed not to accept what your parents called your dowry. They need it to build up the Double B."

"It's better than all the money on earth," Ivy Ann cried, her eyes shining. "Laurel, read it out loud."

Laurel took the single sheet of paper from its envelope and read in an unsteady voice.

Dear Misses Brown,
Your letter made me very happy, more than you can ever know. After much prayer I felt led simply to leave it on my husband's desk. In fear and trembling I waited, hoping and pleading with God that your gentility and beauty of expres-sion and deep love for Adam and

Nathaniel would speak for themselves.

The next day when he left to make a call in the country, I entered his office. My heart sank when I saw how crumpled your letter was, as if a heavy hand had crushed it. In despair I felt all was lost. Then dark, black writing I recognized as my husband's caught my attention. The wrinkled envelope bore the inscription, Numbers 6:24–26.

I hurried to find my Bible, torn between hope and fear. Oh, dear children, the joy that came to me as I read the beautiful words: "The Lord bless thee, and keep thee: The Lord make his face shine upon thee, and be gracious unto thee; The Lord lift up his countenance upon thee, and give thee peace."

Jeremiah has not mentioned your letter nor his response. Yet my prayer of years has been answered and I praise my God and King and offer you this greatest of gifts.

Deepest love from your mother,
Patience Birchfield

Laurel's voice broke on the last words. Diamond drops sparkled in her lashes and in Ivy Ann's. Nat and Adam's strong shoulders bowed before the message that made their wedding day complete.

"The harvest of Mother's faithfulness has come," said Adam, choking on the words.

Laurel's heart lurched at the exalted look in the brothers' faces. *How right it had been to brave a stern father's wrath on behalf of his sons,* she reflected. All the way back to the ranch, through the donning of her bridal white, and even in the midst of the lovely service that gave her into Adam's keeping Laurel treasured that memory. The part of her that was Ivy Ann knew her twin had also tucked it away into her soul, the harvest of faithfulness. How fitting for this November wedding day!

Yet when the last congratulations faded, the final bit of food had been packed away, and Reverend and Mrs. Nathaniel Birchfield slipped away by themselves, Laurel told Adam, "Let's take a walk out of town." She lifted her white skirts, carefully avoiding the ruts made by wagon wheels. After they reached a little rise that gave a splendid view of the darkening sky, the jutting white mountains, and the village she'd come to love, Laurel leaned against Adam's strength. The harvest of love she had so long sought and often despaired of winning lay before her. God grant her wisdom and courage to keep it green and growing in all the seasons of their lives.

ABOUT THE AUTHOR

Colleen L. Reece is a prolific author with over sixty published books. With the popular *Storm Clouds over Chantel,* Reece established herself as a doyenne of Christian romance.